NEVER MIND!

AVI
RACHEL VAIL

NEVER MIND!

A TWIN NOVEL

HARPERCOLLINS*PUBLISHERS*

Never Mind!
Copyright © 2004 by Avi and Rachel Vail
All rights reserved. No part of this book may be
used or reproduced in any manner whatsoever
without written permission except in the case of
brief quotations embodied in critical articles and
reviews. Printed in the United States of America.
For information address HarperCollins Children's
Books, a division of HarperCollins Publishers,
1350 Avenue of the Americas,
New York, NY 10019.
www.harperchildrens.com
Library of Congress Cataloging-in-Publication Data
Avi, 1937–
Never mind! : a twin novel / Avi and Rachel Vail.—
1st ed.
p. cm.
Summary: Twelve-year-old New York City twins
Meg and Edward have nothing in common, so they
are just as shocked as everyone else when Meg's
hopes for popularity and Edward's mischievous
schemes coincidentally collide in a hilarious
showdown.
ISBN 0-06-054314-0
ISBN 0-06-054315-9 (lib. bdg.)
[1. Twins—Fiction. Brothers and sisters—Fiction.
3. Schools—Fiction. 4. New York (N.Y.)—Fiction.
5. Humorous stories.] I. Vail, Rachel. II. Title.
PZ7.A953Ne 2004   2003021439
[Fic]—dc22
Typography by Hilary Zarycky
6 7 8 9 10
❖
First Edition

To Avi
—Rachel

To Rachel
—Avi

1.

EDWARD

● ○

Though my sister, Meg, and I were born on the same day, I *am* ten minutes older, which—trust me—is a lot. True, we have the same parents, live in the same 106th Street apartment, same city, state, country, continent. But I'm *nothing* like her. No way, big way. So I didn't consider myself her *twin*.

Like, in fifth grade we had to interview our grandparents, asking them sixteen questions the teacher handed out. No offense, but our grandparents are not *that* interesting. So I made up new answers. Problem was the teacher didn't believe my grandmother hunted armadillos with a bow and arrow or that my grandfather had the world's largest under-glass ant farm.

Meg did the boring facts. Got an A.

Then there was that time we had to do a report on a favorite animal. Meg wrote about the three-day life of our only pet, a sorry goldfish named Polly. There was nothing to say, really. It lived, it ate, it went belly-up.

I wrote about my pet porcupine, which lived in my closet and chased away burglars. When I read it out

1

loud in class, everyone laughed except Meg . . . and the teacher.

Fortunately, this year my parents figured out a way to send us to *different* middle schools for seventh grade.

"You each have your own talents and styles," Mom said.

"We like it that you're each unusual in your own way," added my dad. "We want to encourage your individuality."

So when seventh grade started—three weeks ago—Meg went to Fischer High on the East Side. I went to Charlton Street Alternative School, downtown.

Meg, as usual, will probably get As in all her classes. An A- or B+ on a quiz means supersulks.

My new school doesn't *give* grades, because they aren't considered meaningful. You pass or fail in small classes where we do lots of projects, field trips, and hands-on stuff. So far, considering that I have to go to school, it seems okay.

Meg isn't just a perfect student. She's also great at sports. She has show-off ribbons (swimming) and trophies (soccer).

I like skateboarding.

Her room is spotless.

My room is a mess.

Meg expects to become a senator. Maybe president. Grown-ups like that. "Good for you," they say. "Like to see that kind of ambition. You've got my vote." Ha ha. Not mine.

If they ask me what I'm going to do, I just say, "Nothing." My hero? Bill Gates. World's richest man—didn't go to college.

Also, Meg looks a lot older than me. She's at least a foot taller—a frigging giantess—and thinks she can look and act like an eighth grader. Ninth, maybe.

Me? The first day of school, Mr. Feffer, the bald teacher with gross hair tufts in his nose, asked me the date of my birth because he wasn't sure I was even *supposed* to be in the seventh grade. That's how puny people think I am. My rat's-tail haircut and fake tattoos don't help.

Also, Meg has six gazillion friends. If she isn't in a crowd, she feels like she's on a desert island. She and her friends talk to each other on the phone all the time. When she hangs up and I ask, "Who was that?" she'll *always* answer, "One of my friends you don't know."

(Of course I *do* know. Because I often listen in on the kitchen extension. My sister may be smart, but she ain't too swift.)

Until this week I had one friend, Stuart Barcaster. While he is the best dude in the world—and worth more than all her friends put together—he was the only one I had.

Get my point? She's twelve noon. I'm midnight. We are that different.

So, then, how can I explain what happened?

2.

MEG

● ○

It all came from trying too hard. That's how I created the whole mess. And what a mess I made this time.

I have always tried too hard. I really try not to, but see? Then I'm trying too hard to not try too hard. My mom got me a book on relaxing last year, but the relaxation exercises stressed me out so much I couldn't get through chapter two. I tell myself to relax a hundred times a day, but then I can't help checking to see if I am relaxed enough and worrying that I am not.

I frighten myself sometimes with what a nutcase I can be. How weird is it that I am the twin who passes for normal?

Mom, I guess, sent in a picture for my new school ID. When my homeroom teacher handed the cards out, I thought I'd gotten somebody else's. Some smiley girl with such a large forehead it's practically a five-head. I recognized the shirt; that was my only tip-off—well, that and my name underneath. Mom says to just be myself, but if I can't even recognize myself in a photograph from last summer, how am I supposed to have any clue who I am?

So I have had to focus on what I do know, which is who I am *not*.

Edward.

I'm not like him at all. It is just a quirk of fate that we shared a womb way back in fetus-hood. We look nothing alike. We act nothing alike. We have absolutely nothing, other than both being twins (coincidentally with each other) in common. My mother even admits it—"The twins are like night and day," she tells people—apologizing, in a way. It's always been pretty clear, even to Edward, which of us is the day.

That is the one thing I can say I definitely have going for me. I am not Edward.

No. I'm just his twin. Which is pretty much the biggest thing I have going against me. (Other than my hair.) But people assume, because we're twins, that Edward is the other half of me. Well, I decided long ago they are dead wrong. Absolutely.

Please, I hope they are wrong.

I have always worried that they were right.

My best friend, Della, has it easy. She never doubts who she is. When people think she is white and ditsy just because she is fair-skinned and cute, she lets them know and fast that she is smart and funny and African American. And for added proof, Della's sister, Ruby, is exactly like her, only six years younger. Ruby is major confirmation that Della is just naturally as good as she seems.

Obviously, since my sibling is less than ideal proof of my value, I had to prove myself some other way.

That's why I took the test for Fischer High School. I studied really hard for it. It's for highly gifted and talented students in grades seven through twelve. (That's what it says on page two of the brochure. I pretty much memorized the application materials. They disintegrated from overhandling with sweaty hands.) That "gifted and talented" stuff put me off it for a while, because the truth is I have no talents or gifts. Not a one. And nothing about me is "highly" either (except my grotesquely gargantuan height). All I have is drive.

Drive is not one of those things they put you on the *Today Show* for, like those three-year-old piano prodigies. "Here's Meg Runyon, copying over her homework—again!" Oh, that would make fascinating reality TV.

I wish I were a naturally gifted something. I'm so not.

When we were little, people thought Edward and I were really smart. Yeah, well, they thought we were blond, too. Turns out we just learned to read early. Eventually everybody caught up and our hair turned brown. But I didn't want to let Mom and Dad down.

I put lemon in my hair and hit the books hard.

Mom says I should lighten up, stop trying so hard to do everything right. Well, yeah, but the problem is, I know what happens when you stop trying: You become Edward.

The day I got the acceptance letter from Fischer was just about the happiest day of my long life. It felt like relief, like freedom, like my chance at a fresh start, my chance to reinvent myself as just me, Meg Runyon.

My ticket away from being the twin of Edward the Onion.

Yeah, well. Turns out that ticket was for one wild ride.

3.

EDWARD

● ○

It began during dinner, when Meg said, "Some kids at my school have started a High Achievers Club."

"What's that all about?" my dad asked.

"To be in the club, you have to be good in everything," Meg explained, all snooty. "Grades, sports, and social life."

"Social life?" my mother said. She put up one eyebrow, a signal that she has questions to ask, but doesn't necessarily ask them—for a while, anyway. "Are you really interested in taking part?" she said.

"I'd like to," Meg said. "I've got the grades, and the sports. I just need to be more helpful in the world. You know, do good deeds in the community. Like helping at nursing homes or at the Red Cross." She smoothed down her hair.

I said, "How about being more helpful to me?"

She made her ugly face. "This has nothing to do with you."

"Meg!" said my mother, defending me.

"So what do you get if you're in this stupid club?" I wanted to know.

She said, "It's being organized by the most popular kids in the whole seventh grade."

"First stop, Snobsville!" I cried.

Dad smiled, reached over, and touched my arm. That's his signal for "You may be right, but don't push it." He likes to act as if he cares for us equally, but I know, deep down, it's really me he prefers. In fact, he said to Meg, "I'm not sure that's a great reason to do all those things."

"It's a question of attitude," my mother agreed.

"But I can try, can't I?" Meg whined.

"Of course," said my mother. "I can see some good things there."

I almost had a fit. *High Achievers Club*. Give me a break! Want to know the only reason she talked about it? To put me down.

So right away I knew there was no way in the frigging world I was going to let my twin sister get into that club. If she did, she would be lording it over me for the rest of my natural life—and beyond.

In other words, my mission was clear: If my twin sister got into that club, it was going to be over my dead body.

In still other words, our heavyweight boxing match, round 6,426. *Gong*.

4.

MEG

● ○

I cleared my plate into the kitchen, trying to decide which member of my family was annoying me the most at that moment. *Snobsville?* Edward can't even be insulting in a normal way. And can Mom please stop smiling at Edward so fake-reassuringly for one minute? But it was Dad who followed me in and pulled on his yellow rubber dishwashing gloves. As I was putting stuff away in the fridge, Dad said, "Meggie, I'm wondering: Why do you want to get into this High Achievers Club? What benefits will it bring you?"

What *benefits*? Oh, right: health insurance and a retirement plan. Hello, it's for *seventh graders*. No wonder I have to claw my way up to normal. Normal is not the native language of my family.

"Dad," I groaned. There was no room in the fridge for the milk. How am I supposed to put things away when they can't possibly fit? (Story of my life.)

"I'm serious," Dad said, tying Mom's gross apron around himself. "Why do you want to get in?"

"I don't even know if I do," I said, realizing I should never have brought up the HAC in the first place. I moved a stack of cream cheesey container things down to a lower shelf.

"You sound nervous about it," Dad commented. The apron was bordered in lace. He looked like a total doofus.

I shoved the milk pitcher in. The handle jutted out. "I probably can't get in anyway. . . ."

"Why not?"

Because you have to do community service and the idea of giving blood or helping old people make flowers out of tissues and pipe cleaners makes me feel like throwing up.

"I don't know." I pushed the milk in and slammed the fridge shut fast.

Something went *snap* inside.

"Fix it," Dad said without missing a beat, adding, "So who are these kids who are starting it? Friends of yours?"

Friends with Kimberly Wu Woodson and Annabelle Jones? The most popular, beautiful, cool girls in seventh grade? I wish.

I leaned against the fridge, hoping nothing would push open the door and crash onto the floor. "I don't know them that well."

"These are the—you said—most popular kids."

I nodded. Is there, in life, worse torture than a heart-to-heart with your father while he is wearing a lacy apron and rubber gloves and the refrigerator is attacking you from behind? I think not.

He turned off the water and leaned back against the sink, pointing a fork at me. "Know the trouble with inside clubs?"

That I'll never get in?

"What?"

"The rest of the world is outside."

Well, duh. "Everybody has an equal chance, Dad," I argued. The fridge door was pressing back at me, so I slid my feet farther away from it for leverage. "Some people don't care, so it's their choice not to try. Some people will try to get in and fail. Some people will get in. No different from trying out for a soccer team. Right?"

Mom came in, carrying her plate and Edward's. (*Edward is so not helpful.*) She was taking deep breaths, something Grandma has advised her to do when Edward is driving her over the edge. I heard about it when I was eavesdropping on their phone call last summer.

"I don't know, Meg," Dad said, shoving his glasses up with his wrist, because of the yellow gloves. I couldn't even look at him anymore.

"Dad, it's not one of those snotty girl cliques that's all about hairstyles and nastiness," I explained. "It's just grades, sports, service. What's wrong with wanting to be inside that?"

It was a summary of every pep talk he's ever given me.

Mom, holding leftover food, stood in front of me. "You know we're proud of you and all your achievements, Meg. We just don't want to rub Edward's face in it. Okay?"

Dad started saying, "That's actually not what I—"

"Okay, Meg?" Mom interrupted.

I blinked at the ceiling, my trick to keep from crying. I never cry. "I might not even get in," I said, confused about which side of the argument I wanted to be on. My parents get me so turned around lately; it is really unfair.

"Of course you will," Mom said, smiling. She kissed me on my forehead. "Can I put this food away?" Mom asked.

What could I do? I stepped away from the fridge. Mom gripped the handle just as the door swung open and all this stuff—including milk—came pouring out.

"Meg!" Mom yelled.

"Nobody around here ever takes me seriously!" I yelled, and ran down the hall to my room, wishing I were allowed to slam my door (family rule number 642). Closing it gently was completely insufficient for the rage I was feeling— though exactly what I was in a rage about I was not so sure.

5.

EDWARD

● ○

That night, in my room, I was playing *Lord of the Rings* on my computer when I got my great idea: If Meg could be part of a High Achievers Club, I'd start a Low Achievers Club. Then we could challenge them to . . . whatever. If we lost, we would be what we were meant to be, *low achievers.* If we won, it would be amazingly awesome. And she would be furious.

In order to be in LAC you'd need to

1. Get grades no higher than just passing
2. Be really bad in team sports
3. Do stuff that really annoys Meg
4. Be called nasty names sometimes
5. Prevent Meg from getting into the High Achievers Club

Cool. I mean, I had four of the five qualifications down pat. I just had to figure out how to do number five. Of course, the one serious problem was I didn't have a lot of friends to make my club big. But I did have my best friend, Stuart Barcaster.

I called him.

"Stu."

"Yeah."

"Ed."

"What's up?"

"Hey, dude, my sister is bugging me."

"Sucks to be you."

"No, really. She's going to be part of this club for stuck-up girls."

"We'll throw you a pity party."

"Actually, I'm going to try to keep her out."

"Why?"

"I want to."

"Go for it."

"Gonna help me?"

"No."

"Why?"

"It's dumb."

"So what? I want to do it anyway."

"Doesn't matter. You're only gonna blow it off."

Stuart's always reminding me that I don't go through with my anti-Meg plots. He says I hatch all these complicated plans to get her and then back out faster than he can eat a bag of Gushers. Which is pretty fast. And also somewhat true.

So I said, "No, I really want to do it."

"Hey, she's your twin sister, not mine."

"Never mind, dude. See you."

"Right."

That, I had to admit, was a big disappointment. But it made me want to deal with this thing more than ever.

So I came up with another idea. I went into what we call the study. It's a room with easy chairs. Books on the wall. (Also, hidden behind, the washer and dryer.) If anyone is sitting in the study reading, you're not allowed to talk (family rule number 245).

When I went into the room, it was just my father who was there, reading a newspaper.

"Can I talk to you?" I asked. That's part of the rule (number 245b)—to ask that—if you find someone reading there.

"Sure," he said, putting his paper down.

"It's this club Meg wants to get into. I think it's stupid."

"Why?"

"It's just a bunch of stuck-up girls," I said.

"I'm not so sure you're right," he said.

I understood *that* to mean that he was leaning toward thinking it *was* a stuck-up thing. He just needed more evidence.

"Look at the way she talks about it," I said.

"Edward, even if what you're saying is true, it's nothing *you* need to worry about. Maybe your mom and I will have to monitor the situation, but . . . well, you are in different schools now. Being separate means you're free to each do your own thing. It's

17

what you both wanted."

That told me they *were* worried about this club and wanted me to stand aside so as not to complicate the situation more.

So I said nothing.

"How's your school going?" he asked.

"Okay."

"Liking it more than your old school?"

I shrugged. "It's school."

"Making some new friends?"

"Stuart."

"He's your old friend."

"He's cool. He's playing drums now."

He took that in for a while.

"So there's nothing nice about it?"

"Has a chess club."

"You in it?"

"It's run by a teacher I hate."

"Who's that?"

"Mrs. Ambruser. The English teacher. She's a weirdo."

"In what way?"

"She laughs too much. And I don't get what she's laughing about. Also, she's always talking about stuff other than what we're supposed to be talking about."

"Does she know what a big fantasy reader you are? That you are an expert on King Arthur?"

"No way."

"Why?"

"She's got her world. I've got mine."

"Edward, all we ask is that you try your best."

"I am," I said with another shrug.

"Cool."

Deciding I'd just have to deal with my sister on my own, I left him.

I was heading back to my room when the phone rang. The trick was I had to race for it. Not that it was for me. Hardly ever is. Probably be for Meg. Which was the whole reason for getting to it first.

"Harry's Pizzeria," I said into the kitchen phone. "How can I help you?"

"Harry's Pizzeria?" came a voice. A girl's voice. I could hardly hear it. She spoke like a two-inch elf with serious laryngitis.

"Sure is," I said. "We deliver in five hours. Plus two minutes more for each additional topping. Sausage. Pepperoni. Tofu tidbits. Tar marbles. Cat hairballs are extra."

"I'm sorry. I must have dialed the wrong number."

She hung up.

And called back ten seconds later.

"Hello?" I said.

"Is Meg there?"

"My twin sister?"

"I didn't know Meg had a twin. What school do you go to?"

"The Manhattan Detention Home for Troubled Boys."

There was a pause. "Is that really true?" she asked in her whispery voice.

"Hey, dude, if it's not true, you get a free cow pie at Harry's Pizzeria. Comes with extra cat hairball toppings."

For a moment she—whoever it was—thought about that. Then, "Can I speak to Meg, please?"

"Who's calling?"

"Kimberly."

"I'm not sure if you are on her A-list of callers."

Another pause. "May I please speak with Meg?"

"Oh yes, yes, please, of course you can!" I cried. "Hang on."

"Meg!" I bellowed. "Phone!"

My sister picked up the phone in the hall.

"It's all right, Edward," she shouted. "I have it. You can hang up."

"Sure," I said. Then I made this click sound with my tongue. You won't believe how hard I practiced that sound. It fools Meg every time. Next I rotated the receiver away from my mouth so she wouldn't hear my breathing.

Then, hoping my folks wouldn't come by, I listened to the whole conversation.

6.

MEG

● ○

I hadn't heard it ring.

That's *it*, I decided. No more music in my room until I'm allowed to get my own phone. Edward is *always* torturing my friends when they call. They try to be nice to him, but he's always saying things like, "Ed's Crematorium. Ash me no questions, I'll tell you who lies."

For him, *annoying* is a synonym for *funny*.

Anyway, I picked up the phone and, figuring it was probably Della, I said, "Hey there." That's what Della and I *always* say.

"Hello?" It was a breathy voice, almost a whisper. Very *not* Della, who is as blunt as baby scissors.

"Hello?" I echoed.

"Is this Meg?"

I could barely hear the voice. I was shoving the phone into my skull, as if the extra millimeter closer to my eardrum might ease things. "Yes?" I said in a strong voice, you know, hinting.

"Hi," she whispered even softer. "This is Kimberly Wu Woodson. From school?"

As if I didn't know who Kimberly Wu Woodson was.

I quickly climbed into my low bookcase, which has a pad on it that I sewed myself to make a reading nook. "Hi," I whispered back. The hint hadn't worked and I didn't want her to think *I* was a big loud jerk. Kimberly Wu Woodson was smart, nice, pretty—basically, the perfect person. I'd been studying her from the first day of school. In fact, she was the reason I'd been getting up half an hour early every morning to do some sit-ups and make my stomach flat like hers and also to try to put together outfits that would be, if not as hip and great looking as hers, at least less schlumpy than my baggy old sweats.

"How are you?" she asked.

Psyched you're calling me, I thought but didn't say. "Fine," I said. "Thanks."

Did she want to talk about the High Achievers Club? She and Annabelle Jones were the kids starting it. I had meant to compliment her on her presentation, but I didn't want to seem suck-uppy. Also there was that problem of service— my inability to do any.

"Um," I said, pondering whether to mention it. Maybe she just called to chat. So, not wanting to sound overanxious, I tried to think of some funny thing that might've happened at lunch I could mention. She and I usually sat at the same table—opposite ends—when she stayed at school for lunch, though she was one of the chatters and I was one of the stare-into-her-lunch-bag-and-try-not-to-embarrass-myself-ers.

She was also in my science class. Maybe she wanted the

homework? I jumped up to get my assignment pad, just in case. On my way I smacked my head into the top of my book nook. The impact of the head clonk caused me to drop the phone. When I picked it up, she was saying, "I'm fine too."

"Oh, good," I said, too enthusiastically, and then covered my eyes, thinking, *I am hopeless*. As if she'd been ill or something. *Think! Say something!* "Um," I said again, brilliantly. "So . . ."

But before I could come up with anything, she asked, "Do you really have a twin brother?"

Groan. Edward must have mentioned the nasty fact of his existence to Kimberly when he picked up the phone. I sank down onto my bed. "Um . . ."

My plan to keep Edward a total secret had been beautifully simple: never mention he existed. I had been pretty proud of that strategy. I figured, it's not like anybody would ask, out of the blue, *What's your name? Where did you go to school before? Do you have a twin brother?*

I just hadn't worked out all the kinks, like, what if he happened to answer the phone and say, "Hi, this is Meg's weirdo twin brother."

"Meg?"

I had to say something. I came up with "I, well, if, I mean . . ."

There was a pause, long enough for me to think, *Well, isn't that a brilliant way out of the problem? How articulate! Oh, yes, I must truly be gifted.*

"I didn't know you were a twin," Kimberly said. "I'm fascinated by twins."

"Oh," I said. "Well, yes, I'm a twin. So, um, Kimberly— that was interesting, that High Achievers—"

"But your twin isn't at Fischer with us, is he? I'm sure I would've . . ."

"No," I said, getting that familiar sick feeling in my stomach. "He's not. But anyway . . ."

"Oh," whispered Kimberly. "Didn't he get in?"

Which actually meant *you just squeaked by* in most people's ridiculous logic about twins. Great. That's exactly what I mean: He always drags me down. Well, this time, it was *not* going to happen. "No," I blurted out. "That isn't it."

"What is it then?" she asked. "He said something about going to a . . . detention home for troubled boys?"

Good idea. Too bad it's not true. "Is that what he said?" I managed a dismissive laugh.

"You okay?"

The laugh apparently was unconvincing. "Yes. No. He's just got such a great sense of humor." Sure.

"Oh. So where does he go?"

There was no way I could tell her Charlton Street Oddball School without totally obliterating my future social life. "The, um . . . he, well, it's this really special . . . I don't know if you would've heard of it. . . ."

"I bet I have," Kimberly said, sounding insulted.

"No," I stammered, impressing myself with my ability to screw up an important conversation with every single word.

"It's not, no, it's just . . ."

"What, is he, like, a genius in something?"

"Uh . . ." *Okay. Thank you for the idea. Genius is better than idiot.* "Well, sort of," I said.

"Meg, we're both at Fischer. You don't have to go all humble."

"Well, I just don't want people to think I'm bragging," I said humbly.

"I know," Kimberly said. She actually sighed. "I'm the same way. People are *always* asking me about my tennis ranking or my academic achievements. I get *so* uncomfortable. I mean, how can you say the truth without making people feel inferior and jealous?"

Oh, yeah. I have the same problem. Such a bother hiding all my many talents from people.

She laughed, though, so I laughed along. Mine sounded like *haw, haw,* so I stopped.

"But you can tell me," she whispered. "Don't worry about it. I can tell you're not stuck-up like some people. What kind of genius is he? Musical?"

Okay. Why not? "Ah . . . right," I said. "Musical."

"He doesn't go to the New York Musical Conservatory, does he?" she asked, gasping. "That is *so* hard to get into. Does he really?"

"Well," I said, "actually, yes. The, ah, Musical Conservatory." It was almost funny. Edward can't even hum on key.

"Wow," she said. "Even *I* didn't get in there, and I'm all-city in flute. I got wait-listed, which is still really selective, but wow. I don't know anybody who's gotten in there."

"No?"

"No, nobody."

Phew! Lucky break. I could feel myself sliding into a pit. But before I could grab hold of something, she said, "What does he play? I mean, besides piano. I know you have to be amazing on piano and at least one other instrument to get into MC."

"Oh," I said, trying to remember if she played any instrument besides piano and flute. I didn't want anything near flute, for sure. Or she'd have to know him from all-city, maybe, whatever that is.

"Meg?" she prompted.

"Bass, um . . ." I almost said bass fiddle, but I was pretty sure the twin sister of someone who played such a thing would not call it that. What was the real name of that thing bigger than a cello? I could've just said cello, in fact, should've. But I wanted to make Edward haul some big-ass bulky thing around the city as punishment for getting me into this.

"Bass?" asked Kimberly. For a second I thought I'd really blown it—gotten so involved in the mechanics of Edward's imaginary life I'd forgotten to finish saying what instrument he was supposedly gifted at.

I was about to say, "Oh, yeah, that's what all the kids at—whatever the name of that school was you mentioned—call their cellos, they're so brilliant and cool."

"Oh, right," she cut me off just in time. "Bass. For a

second I thought you meant bass guitar. Like in a jazz band or rock group. I'm so stupid." Kimberly laughed a really cute little self-deprecating giggle. In my assignment pad I wrote: *Develop cute self-deprecating giggle.* If I could make the travel soccer team, I can learn to giggle. Self-deprecatingly.

"No, you're not stupid at all," I said generously. "He plays bass guitar, too. As well as usual guitar." *What the heck, as long as I was loading up Edward with talents . . ."* Actually, he and a few of his friends have a band."

"A band! Oh, wow," she said.

"Yeah." If Edward could be a brilliant musician, why shouldn't he have friends, too? It's not that much more far-fetched.

"That's so cool," Kimberly whispered. "Must be fun for you."

"Yeah." I could feel myself beginning to get a little annoyed with Kimberly. How gullible and easily impressed can a supposed High Achiever be? No, that's mean, I told myself. Maybe a nice, honest person would have no reason to think I was totally, randomly *lying*.

"He sounded so cool on the phone before," Kimberly went on. "You know, when I was talking with him. Edgy. Not like your typical seventh-grade boy—so mature. Am I right? And funny, too."

"Yeah," I said. "He's really funny." Depending which meaning of *funny* you're using, I'd finally said something that was true.

"Listen," Kimberly whispered, "my mom is gonna make me get off the phone in a sec. I was going to ask if you wanted to come over for a party. It's this Saturday night."

"Sure," I said, too quickly, interrupting her. Why can't I ever just chill?

"Great," she said. "Why don't you bring your brother and his friends? It's going to be boy-girl, anyway. They could even, maybe, play for us."

Uh-oh. "Um . . ."

Kimberly yelled, "Okay! Okay! I'm getting off!"

I dropped the phone again, from the shock of the volume.

When I got it to my ear again, she was back to whispering. "My mom is so on my case lately. Does yours ever drive you nuts?"

"Lately, yeah," I admitted.

"Good," she whispered. "So it's not just me."

"Definitely not," I said, smiling. Della gets along perfectly with her mom.

"Good," said Kimberly. "Don't say anything to anybody."

"Okay," I said, though I wasn't sure what not to say—that her mom drives her nuts? That mine drives me nuts? About her party? But for once, I kept my mouth shut.

"Well," she said, "let me know in school tomorrow."

"Okay," I said, smiling more. Let her know what? Well, whatever.

"Bye. Oh, wait," she said. "What's his name?"

"Whose?"

"Your brother."

"Oh." Him? Bleh. "Edward."

"Edward?" His name sounded like an accusation in her voice. *Edward?* It sounded far from the cool, brilliant, rock/classical bass player I had conjured up and very close to, well, Edward.

"But we call him Ted," I actually heard myself say.

"Ted Runyon," she said. "Wow. He really does *sound* like a rock star."

"Yeah, well, sure . . . Exactly. A rock star," I mumbled. "Bye."

"Bye!"

She hung up, except I thought I heard her laughing. Was that possible?

But I had no time to stress about losing my mind. I had to figure out what my incredibly awesome fantasy brother Ted was doing Saturday night so that he could *not*—repeat *not*—under any circumstances—*could not* go to Kimberly's party.

7.

EDWARD

● ○

Though I had heard the whole conversation, I still couldn't believe it. Meg had given me the whole thing—the perfect way to keep her out of that stupid High Achievers Club—right in my lap. Me, a *musician*! A bass player! With a band! Too cool! And my new name, Ted. Way to go, Meg!

Quick as anything I dialed star-six-nine. The phone company robot voice said, "The-number-that-most-recently-called-was five-five-five-six-eight-nine-zero. For-an-additional-thirty-five-cents-we-will-connect-you-to-this-number."

I wrote the number down. Sooner or later I'd have to call this Kimberly if this was going to work.

But I had to figure out what I was going to do first. I actually started to pace around my room, trying to figure it all out. I was so hyped!

The first thing I decided to do was make up a band. Then I'd call Kimberly and tell her that we—the band—*would* show up at her stupid Saturday party. I knew she would believe it too. If I have learned one thing, it's this: Smart people can be so dumb. Then, when we showed up, it would embarrass Meg so much that she could forget all about being in that club with that no-voiced elf.

So easy!

Next thing I did was check to make sure Meg would not be on the phone, which I did by going into her room. She was sitting in her bookcase doing her homework. This place, her bookcase, believe it or not, was what she called her "reading nook."

(Now seriously, as if normal people ever used the word *nook*. I asked my mother what *nook* meant and she said I should look it up. Knowing I can't spell, she added "n-o-o-k." So I had to look it up and the book said, "A corner of a quadrilateral or angular figure bounded by straight lines." Which told me exactly nothing—which is probably why Meg used the word in the first place. She stuffs words into sentences the way other people stuff sausages for a living.)

"Hey, who was that who called before?" I asked my dear twin sister.

"One of my friends you don't know," she said. If you think the moon is predictable, try my sister.

"Maybe I do know her."

"Edward, trust me, you don't. Now go away; I'm busy with homework, okay?"

"She someone special?" I asked, enjoying myself more than she could guess.

"Edward, she's like the top. . . . Believe me, you

don't know her and you wouldn't like her if you did" was the answer. "Okay? Now would you *please* leave me alone? Some of us like to get good grades."

"Yeah, right. For the High Achievers Club."

"Edward, in normal school kids get homework and you have to do it. It's not necessarily fun, but that's why they don't call it home-have-fun-pestering-people. Just home*work*. Get it?"

"Uh . . . ," I said, sounding as stupid as possible.

"Oh, man! Do you know what you are?" she said.

I opened my eyes as wide as possible and shook my head, like *Please, Miss Wonderful, tell me who I am because I am so stupid I don't even know.*

She looked away and grumbled, "Never mind."

"Really? Never mind? Is that what I am?" I asked. "A never mind?" After which I left her in her corner quadrilateral or angular figure bounded by straight lines.

I went into my room and punched my punching bag a few times to calm down.

When I was done, I decided the first thing I had to do was think up a name for the band. That was so important. See, it had to sound right—real and totally mysterious. Except it also had to make sense when they thought about it later.

Actually, I didn't know too much about music, but I knew some famous names. So the first names for my band popped up into my head quick:

The Grateful Bed
The Rolling Phones, or Rolling Phonies
You Also
In Stink
M & M

Even I had to admit those names were lame. So I made myself sit down and think real hard. What was like . . . me? And what I finally came up with was:

Never Mind

The more I thought about it, the more I liked it. Like, never mind, you fools, there's no band after all. Like, I never mind you people anyway, so who needs you? And maybe even like, you should never use your minds so much, you stuck-up, smarty-pants jerks. And just forget it, never mind, dismissed. Like Meg just did to me. So, yeah, Never Mind. That Meg supplied the name would be part of my revenge.

I raced to the phone and dialed Kimberly's number.

"Hello," came a loud voice. "Kimberly Wu Woodson's private secretary."

Pitching my voice as low as I could get it, I said, "Can I speak to Kimberly?"

"Yeah."

"Is that you?" I asked. Then I heard, "Brett, give me that phone!" Then, "Hello?" It was Kimberly for sure with that voice that sounded like it was smothered by used and loaded snot tissues.

"Is this Kimberly?" I was trying to sound loud and confidant.

"Yes. Who's this?"

"Ted Runyon. Meg's twin brother."

For a moment she didn't say anything. Then, "Oh!" in a voice that got softer. "Ted? The *musician*?"

"You got it, baby." I have always wanted to say that to a girl.

"Oh! Wow. Hi."

"Hi," I said, and then held off, so she would have to figure out what I was up to.

"I mean, wow," she actually said again. And I thought *I* was the world's biggest loser. "So, um . . . ," she added.

I said, "My sister has talked a lot about you. She said you're the top."

"The top what?"

Fool, I thought, but didn't say.

"My sister also just told me that you're having a party this Saturday and would be way interested in having my band play at it." My voice sort of broke midway, but I got it back down.

"She did?"

"We wouldn't charge you or anything," I said. "You probably couldn't afford us anyway. We get thousands."

"Oh, well—"

"But," I rushed on, "see, we're working on a new CD and, you know, this would give us a chance to try it out for some kids."

"Oh, wow."

"Could you repeat that?" I said, grinning.

"I mean . . . you would really come?"

"Yeah, sure. I'd do anything for my twin sister. We're very close. Love her, love me. Love me, love her."

"Oh, wow," she said again, beginning to sound like a puppy who needed to go out. "That's so . . . she's . . . Wow."

I said, "I'll get the details from Meg."

"*Thank* you. Can I ask—I guess I should know what it is—but, can you tell me what your band's name is?"

"Never Mind."

"Well, I just thought it would be nice to know. So I can tell everybody."

I had to smile. So good. "No, that's the name of the band. *Never Mind*. Get it?"

"Oh." She giggled. "I really am dim, huh? Please don't think this is how I am."

"How are you?"

"Fine."

"I meant . . ."

"I know. Joke. Anyway, sorry. Never Mind. What a cool name for a band."

"You like it?"

"Oh, yeah," she said. "It sounds, familiar, actually. Could that be possible?"

"Anything's possible." I never had sounded so cool before. In fact, I never actually talked to a girl on the phone before. Being Ted was so much better than being me.

"Yeah," she whispered.

Neither of us said anything for a moment. I was starting to think maybe she'd hung up, that maybe I was turning into Edward again. You know, Dr. Jekyll, Mr. Hide-under-the-bed. I almost hung up myself, but then she said, "Ted?"

"Yeah?" Yeah, that's me. Ted.

"Do you two—you know, you and Meg—do you look alike?"

"I'm taller," I said. "Bigger. I can pass for sixteen."

"Oh . . ."

"Wow," I filled in, and hung up, grinning so much it's a wonder my teeth didn't spill out onto the floor.

So I punched my punching bag to calm down again. In fact, the hard part of the evening was not telling Meg what I'd done.

"What are you grinning about?" she asked when we passed in the hall.

"I'm not grinning," I said. "I'm just keeping in a belch." Which I pumped out right then.

"That's *not* funny," she screamed at me.

Except it was funny. Very funny.

8.

MEG

● ○

A loft downtown, I doodled on my notebook, bumping in the aisle seat as I went toward school the next morning. At the next bus stop I made tight circles over it, blotting it out. A girl from my science class, Esther Grossbart, got on the bus. I'd never seen her on my bus before. I smiled and moved over, but she walked right by and sat with another girl from my school. Worse, a very large man with five stuffed shopping bags plopped himself down into the newly empty seat beside me. I decided not to care. I needed the time on the bus to myself—to focus, give myself a pep talk, make my plan for the day. If only the fat man didn't cough quite so much.

A loft in Soho—that's where, I decided, my famous brother and his band pals were going to a party Saturday night. Or maybe playing at a loft downtown. Either way, unfortunately, they *would not* be able to come to Kimberly's party.

But, hey, maybe another time.

Maybe another universe.

As the bus approached school, I realized I had overlooked one critical element: Edward's band's name. Or rather, Ted's.

I picked up my backpack and squeezed past Cough Man. What would be a good name for a band as cool as Ted's? Nothing was coming to me. I followed Esther Grossbart down the steps, wondering if she realized I was there and wanted to walk together. She didn't. She seemed, actually, like someone with no sense of humor and probably a very politically correct opinion about makeup, even for those of us who really need it.

But I had no time for her anyway. *Band name. Band name.*

Nothing. Sometimes my brain is so dull it shocks me I can even get into my shoes, never mind a gifted school. Never mind get *out* of a stupid lie. *Why did I get myself into this?*

Maybe I could just tell Kimberly, Hey, never mind what I said last night about my cool twin brother and his band because, see, they all flew off to, maybe, um, Japan for the year, suddenly this morning. Right. There had to be limits even to her gullibility. By then I was already past the main office. *Think!* I told myself. *Just think of a name!*

I was getting so desperate I even considered honesty. I could just say, "Never mind the band, there's no band, there's no Ted, there's just Edward."

Yeah, right. Honesty was not among my choices when it came to explaining Edward.

I couldn't help picturing him as he stood there last night, his innocent eyes all wide, dreading and waiting for the answer to "Do you know what you are?" I was so mad right then I almost slipped and said it. But I stopped myself. Though when I said "Never mind," he acted like that was insulting enough.

And that's how it came to me, the perfect name for his band:

Never Mind

The minute I thought of it, I loved it. No one but me, of course, would fully appreciate the real humor of it, but it was *so* perfect. Never Mind, the band (because—there is no band!). Never mind what I say, because I lie. Never mind that puny little weird boy who says he's my twin. Never care, never worry, never bother, never pay attention, never think, never take offense. Never mind. *Yes!*

Meg Runyon, I said to myself, *sometimes you actually are gifted*.

I was getting into it. I wandered down the hall, picturing "Ted." He'd be so different from Edward in every way. He'd be tall—taller than me, totally unlike Edward. He'd also have big, white, straight teeth (Edward has braces) and an easy smile, straight blond hair that he wears a little long, since he's a musician. Or maybe even a ponytail? Nah, that's too cliché. Just a little overgrown. I guess he'd be sort of on the skinny side, that sort of wastie musician type—though maybe Ted is a jock, too, a casual jock. He plays tennis, I think—nah, too country club, and it's what Kimberly does. She wouldn't play soccer. Never. Too dirty.

Okay. So soccer. But not an only-play-when-way-in-the-lead backup goalie like me—a midfielder, because he's such an all-around kind of guy, a team player. And though he has a million friends and even more hangers-on, he'd really rather spend his time jamming with his band or just hanging out with me—his twin sister and (why not?) best friend.

I was just thinking how it's too bad he's so dedicated to his music that he had to turn down going to Fischer with me, when I got to my locker and realized the small crowd there was waiting for—oh, no—me.

"Hi," I said, snapping out of my imaginary world the way my father comes to stops at lights, screeching and jolting.

"Hi," said Annabelle, chewing her gum. "So. That is so cool."

I looked from face to face. These were the most popular seventh-grade girls, crowding around me, looking at me. It was not a situation I wanted to screw up. You don't want to presume to know what's going on and do the wrong thing, but you also don't want to seem oblivious to something that's obvious to everybody else. I tilted my head just a bit. It's something Della does. It can mean whatever somebody thinks it should mean.

"About your brother," Kimberly said.

"Oh," I said, trying to sound full of regret.

"Playing at Kimberly's party," added Annabelle.

"Oh," I said again, but this time *actually* full of regret.

"He seems a lot less . . ." Kimberly looked around at the

other girls, as if searching for the word she wanted on their faces. She turned back to me and I guess saw the word she needed: "Shy. Less shy than you. No offense."

I tried to smile. I couldn't quite make my mouth muscles go up. "He's a bit of a goof," I said, trying out Kimberly's self-deprecating giggle. It sounded like a donkey braying. I cleared my throat and added, "On the phone."

Kimberly's face got serious. "I didn't think so. But I've only talked to him twice."

"Yeah," I started, then stopped. *Twice? She talked to him twice?*

"What's the band's name again?" Annabelle asked.

Before I could answer, Kimberly said, "Never Mind."

"What?" I gasped.

"It is *so* cool," she said. "I can't believe Never Mind is really playing at my party!"

The other girls were actually squealing.

I was confused. To put it mildly. Had she read my mind? Had I told her somehow and forgotten? How could she know the name I'd invented—two minutes earlier—for my imaginary brother's imaginary band? And what did she mean, twice? I figured she had to have talked to him once when he had answered the phone. Did she call a second time?

Before I could work that out, Kimberly scrunched her nose and whispered in my ear, "I think I'm falling in love with your twin brother!"

She squeezed my arm, then walked away surrounded by

the other whispering girls.

In total disbelief I watched them go. They swished down the hall toward our class. My lunch bag fell on the floor. I bent over to pick it up and banged my head on my lock, which I don't think I could've done if I'd been trying.

Never Mind?

How did they guess that?

9.

EDWARD

● ○

Wednesday morning, as Dad and I took the subway downtown—he to work, me to school—I was in such a silent funk he leaned toward me and over the roar asked, "Are you upset about something?"

"Just sleepy," I said, which is one of my fake outs for not wanting to talk. I was hot and uncomfortable. Seemed like the whole city was packed in our subway car—like five pounds of cold spaghetti in a one-pound bowl.

"Late-night computer games?"

"I suppose."

He took me seriously, because he said, "I think you need to ease off, then. How about no games after eight thirty?"

"Okay."

"Really?" He seemed surprised I gave in so quick.

"Sure."

He left it at that, which was good, because in fact I had woken upset about what I had done. I mean about Meg and all. The whole thing I had cooked up—the rock band. Okay: it *was* very funny when I had talked it up on the phone with this stupid friend of Meg's, this Dim Kimberly girl. She loved Never Mind and all that. Only by the next morning it was beginning to sink in that now I had to *do* it.

The problem was, I began to worry that maybe it was *me* who was being set up. That is, the more I thought about it, the more it was pretty hard to believe that this Dimberly was actually stupid enough to believe, one, all that stuff my sister had said about me, and, two, all that stuff that I had told her. She was supposed to be Talented and Gifted, right? Not Totaled and Goofy.

Maybe, I started thinking, *Meg had figured out that I was listening to her calls, and this whole thing was her way of getting back at me.*

That is, maybe Meg said to Kimberly, "I need to play a trick on my brother."

Maybe it was Meg's way to lure me to this dumb party just to embarrass me. The way she had those times when she held her nose when she went past me in our old school. The *onion* thing.

A kind of an ambush. That was bad.

I was getting a little freaked about what I had started rolling down the hill. Of course, I kept telling myself that I didn't have to go on. I mean, I was *not* Ted Runyon, rock star. There was no band called Never Mind. No way, big way. I was Edward Runyon, the immature, runty underachiever. I could put on the brakes, say never mind. No problem, right?

Dad got off at his stop, Thirty-fourth Street, and I went on to school. The crowd peeled off as we headed downtown. I could breathe again. I just wasn't sure I wanted to.

During the first recess at school (we get a lot of recess—it's called "Creative Exercise"), I got into a huddle with Stuart.

It was a small huddle because Stuart is seriously small. I mean, that's just the way he is. Remember, while I'm taller than he is, I'm not so tall myself. Not like my Empire State Building sister. He's also sort of chubby and keeps his hair long down his neck.

His weird father (he's a fish sniffer in a fish-processing factory—honest) and his mother got divorced, and he has this stepfather who is a high school math teacher geek who is always trying to get Stu to like math. Stu's a bit bummed out about it all. I mean, it's hard enough to figure life out, never mind algebra.

Here's a true story about Stuart. Once he was with me and my mom. We were walking up Central Park West toward the Tavern on the Green playgrounds. Anyway, we met this friend of my mom's, and the lady has a big dog. So while she's standing there talking to this lady, the dog comes up to Stu, sniffs him up and down, then lifts his leg on him and . . . *pees*.

Honest. It was so funny, except . . . it wasn't. And Stuart doesn't even like dogs. But that's the kind of guy he is.

He's really pale and wears glasses. The way I figure it, he can't see much without them, but he leaves them in odd places and, not seeing, he sits on them—a lot. That makes them the most whacked eyeglasses in the whole universe. So when Stuart actually does find his glasses and puts them on, it looks like he's got one eye higher than the other. It's not him, of course, it's the glasses. Just lopsided, that's all.

But he is a pretty good skateboarder.

Now the thing is, like I said before, Stuart also plays the drums. So naturally, since he is my best friend, and he is a musician—sort of—I told him what I had done. The band business, I mean.

"You really said all that stuff to the girl?" he said to me. He was digging into his brown paper snack bag like he was searching for gold.

"Yeah."

"And she really believed it?"

"Yeah."

"And her name is really Dimberly?"

"Actually, Kimberly."

"Too bad. Dimberly. I like that."

"Stuart . . ."

"And you really told her you were going to go to her party and do this band?"

"Yeah."

"And your sister doesn't know?"

"No way."

"What's the name of this band?"

"Never Mind."

"Just asking."

"No, that's the band's name. *Never Mind.*"

He considered me through those crooked glasses of his while he mashed a large and somewhat melted chocolate-covered Krispy Kreme doughnut into his mouth—or at least most of it into his mouth. A lot was in his lap and on his lips. And his cheeks. Even one ear. It was as if he had stuck his face in a mud pile.

"You are weird," he finally said when he could speak, though his mouth was still packed full—which meant a few crumbs came my way.

"And proud of it," I said.

"What's the point?" Stuart asked, his *p* propelling even more crumbs—missilelike—in my direction.

I shrugged. "It'll be so funny," I said, trying to convince myself as much as him. "And it would embarrass Meg."

"And this time do you really intend to do it?"

"Swear."

He started chomping on a second doughnut. "You know, you could just leave it alone. You. Her. Two people. Different. Get it?"

"Forget it," I said.

"Hey, cry me a river, build a bridge, and get over it," he said.

"Come on," I said. "We could do this . . . gig. There

would be all this food, and girls. . . ."

That must have got him because he looked around. "What kind of food?" he said.

"You know, party food. I think this Dimberly is rich. Gotta be all you can eat."

"How do you know she's rich?"

"I don't know. Sounds like it."

"Would we eat, you know, before or after we played?"

"Both. Promise. What do you say?"

"*This* Saturday night?"

"Yeah."

"I'm supposed to do something with my father."

"But he never shows up, right?"

He gave me a dirty look. "Shut up."

"Okay."

Next moment he said, "You know what my dad does?"

"Sniffs for bad fish in a . . . fish factory."

"Right, and weekends he needs to get into clear air— you know, away from the city—so his nose can . . . revive."

"Sure."

He was silent for a moment. Then he said, "This party—promise you're not gonna pull a U-ey at the last minute?"

"No way," I said.

"I think I know some other guys who could play."

"Really?" I didn't think Stuart had any friends besides me.

"Yeah," he said.

"Cool."

He nodded. "How we going to get my drum set to wherever this is?"

"I'll figure something out."

"Get us rides? There and back?"

"Yeah."

"You sure?"

"Yeah."

"And you're really, totally, altogether in? Not backing out?"

"Yeah."

"You know what?" he said.

"What?"

"Ever hear of the SATs?"

"Yeah."

"You need to work on your vocabulary. *Yeah* isn't going to be enough."

"You'll do it?" I asked, wanting to be sure I was hearing him right.

He looked at me with a bit of a crooked smile that went perfect with his crooked glasses and said, "Yeah."

"That's my word."

He broke into a full grin. "Yeah."

10.

MEG

● ○

The rest of the day, all people wanted was to chat about my twin brother, Ted, and his band.

How many of them are in the band? ("Four," I said.)

What are they like? ("Oh," I said, "a lot like Ted, only not quite as much, sometimes. But, you know, of that type." They actually nodded at that. These people are gifted?)

What are their names? "Um . . ."

Nothing came to me. I couldn't think of one boy name, not one. This was at lunch, standing out in the courtyard. I was surrounded.

"Their names?" repeated Annabelle. "Hello!"

I looked at my watch and gasped and said, "Oh, my— speaking of those guys—sorry—I have to—be right back." I ran across the courtyard, pressed against the heavy metal door, and, without looking back, slipped inside the school. I took a breath and decided it wasn't safe to stay right inside the door. I looked around and chose the steps—I'd go up, down the hall, around by the office, make a phone call. Yeah. Urgent phone call. Can't believe I forgot.

Nobody stopped me or asked for my hall pass. I got to the phone and found the right coins in my pocket, deposited them, and only then thought, *Who should I call?* I decided to call home. I could always leave a message on the machine. That way, if somebody came by, I could make it sound like I was really talking to somebody. Then, when I got home, I would erase it.

It was smart of me to have thought of actually calling, because just as our message was finishing, who should come down the hall but the whole pack of girls, my new best friends.

"Hey!" one of them, the one whose name I could never remember, was yelling to me and waving.

I turned my back to them and just started talking randomly. "Uh-huh! Yeah, definitely. No, Ted said he would— hmmm? Yeah. Ted. Uh-huh. So I'll go with Ted. Who else would I want to go with? Right? Ted. Mm-hmm, right, well, they'll bring, you know, their, um, own instruments. Ted, Rick, Joe, and . . . Jeremiah."

The girls were passing me then, and the boy names came to me in a rush. Well, Rick and Joe did. Jeremiah I figured could be the drummer. I raised my eyebrows at the swarm as they paused, then passed. I managed a small smile, very much like Kimberly's. It must have worked because she flashed one back at me.

I heard Annabelle saying, "Rick, Joe, Jeremiah—so cute!"

I pretended I was listening intently to whatever the person I had to call so urgently was telling me, because I felt pretty tapped out of imagination for the day. The machine beeped and hung up. Hung up on by my own answering machine. How truly pathetic.

Things got worse. Because though I managed to be late to class for the second time in the day (and in my life), in order not to have to answer any more questions, what I found there was a paper on my desk. It looked like this:

High Achievers Club

(If you want to be considered for the club, fill out this form completely and hand it in to Kimberly or Annabelle before first period tomorrow.)

Name _____

My scores on the last three quizzes/homeworks in:

Math	Science	Eng.	SS
1.			
2.			
3.			

My teams:

sport	position	awards	record
1.			
2.			
3.			

My public service activities:

1.

2.

3.

Why I think I should be considered for this club (essay):

But what was even worse, in faint pencil—like a whisper—was this note on the bottom of the page:

Meg—don't worry. It'll be fun.

☺

You know you're in! Call me later.
Kimberly

What did that mean? Don't worry because she knows somehow that I have nothing to put for community service? Or that she has confidence I'll find some to do? Or was I automatic, without doing any good in the world, without any of those qualifications I had told Dad were the whole point?

So *was* it a snotty girls club after all? Forget being smart, athletic, and good—I wasn't even getting in by being a cool and nasty girl myself, but because of my brother. I got in because of *Edward*!

No, that could not be it. And Kimberly and Annabelle were not snotty and nasty. They were nice, sweet, friendly, warm, pretty, and polite—everything I wish I could be, including smart and confident.

Or—maybe—they just liked me.

No, not me. It was my glamorous (though imaginary) twin they liked.

Unable to concentrate, I stared at the girl from the bus, Esther Grossbart. Is there a more unfortunate name? (I could guess what Edward would call her.) She is the type of person Della had teased me I was going to have to end up friends with if I went to Fischer—an intellectual nerd. I was like, No way. I didn't have to be friends with Esther Grossbart; I could be friends with Kimberly and Annabelle, who were at least as cool as Della.

Though Della wouldn't like them. She can't stand overly cheerful people. "Sitcom-smilers," she calls them.

Call Della, I wrote in my notebook.

I studied Esther Grossbart some more. Other than her pen and her eyes, she barely moved. But then she picked up the High Achievers Club application. I watched her skim it, fold it twice, rip it neatly down the folds, and then stack the pieces in the corner of her desk.

And I knew why. Because she knew she could never get in. And she accepted that she'd never get into the club, even if she could overflow the lists in every category.

Why? Because everybody knew there was an unlisted category.

If it was called anything, which it is emphatically *not*, it would be called something like Coolness Rating.

In that unlisted, understood category, the CR, Esther Grossbart would have a zero. I wasn't thinking that to be mean. In fact, as I sat and studied her, the truth is I started envying her even more than I envy Della, normally, or Kimberly and Annabelle, lately. Esther Grossbart knew her place. Which I guess she had in common with Della, Kimberly, and Annabelle—though it's a different place, she definitely knew where she did and didn't fit in.

Unlike me.

No. More likely it was that she *knew* she couldn't get in. If she didn't care, it had to be that she convinced herself she didn't care because she knew she couldn't get it—the old sour grapes thing. Right?

Or maybe, I thought, *maybe Esther did not even want to get into the club.* Could that be? That would make Esther Grossbart cooler than the cool people, right? But no, that doesn't make sense, and anyway, who cares about Esther? Back to my main subject: me.

What was *my* Coolness Rating? No idea. So where did I fit? No clue. How completely, devastatingly uncool. My only hope was to keep anyone from finding out the truth.

Later, as I rode home on the bus, staring at the High Achievers sheet, the hardest homework I've ever gotten, a crazy thought hit me: Ted, my imaginary brother, knew where he fit in, of course, which was at the top of any social crowd he wants—but my actual brother, who was otherwise the opposite of Ted, understood his place, too. He was at the bottom, but at least he knew it. And he didn't mind.

At that moment I was almost envying *him.*

Then I remembered his face, last year, during the worst of it. How angry he looked at the other kids when they held their noses when he went by, all "Ew, do you smell something? It's Runyon the onion!" But worse, how he looked at me when I did exactly the same thing. Well, how could I not? They were starting to do it to me, too, hold their noses when they had to sit next to *me*—I *had* to separate myself. I am *not* an onion. But Edward didn't growl at me the way he did at them. He just looked, well, surprised. And sad.

No, I decided—as discombobulating as it is to be me, I don't wish I could trade places and let myself be a loser like Edward. I would never let myself get stomped on the way he did, the way I had stomped on him.

It's better to be mean than to be hurt.

Isn't it?

So that's what I was thinking all the way home and down the steps of the bus when we got to my stop, which is why I didn't notice who was waiting there until I practically bumped into her.

Mom.

She grabbed me. "Meg," she said.

"Mom? What's wrong? Why aren't you at work? Did something happen?"

"That's what I'd like to know. Meg," she said, dead serious. "I need to know the truth about what's going on."

11.

EDWARD

● ○

I was still thinking maybe I should find a way to get out of the whole Kimberly party thing during second recess when I felt a tap on my shoulder. I looked around. These two huge eighth graders were standing there. I mean those guys were *big*. I only knew them by name: One was called Albert Delongi. The other was Tommy Pennypacker.

Albert was this tall skinny guy, with the kind of blotchy zit-dipped skin that people call "pebble face." As if to hide it, he had one long, dyed-green strand of hair that came down till it reached his pointy chin, which had some blond fuzz on it. Tell the truth, he looked like a reject peach in the bruised fruit section of the supermarket.

As for Tommy, he was this dark guy who wore his clothes so loose he was like a hot air balloon in search of gas. He didn't say much that I ever heard, but he always *looked* very serious. Aside from having his hair in dreads, he also had this wisp of a goatee on his chin—sort of like the shadow of what he might have when he got to be forty—not fourteen, which he actually was.

The two of them always hung together like a living yin and yang sign.

"What's up, man," Albert said to me.

"Not much," I said.

"Hey, man," Tommy said, "Stuart Barcaster said you were starting up a band."

"He did?"

"Yeah. Thing is, I play the bass. Tommy here is on guitar. We're not too bad. Been looking for a band, man. What do you play?"

"Not much."

"Lead singer, eh?"

"I guess . . . ," I said, though that was news to me.

"Anyway, dude," Albert went on, "Stuart said you got a gig lined up for this Saturday night. Him and us, we play together up in his building. Know what I'm saying? Thirty-third floor?"

I nodded, without having any idea what he was talking about.

"So," he went on, after some mysterious, meaningful looks with his friend, "if you can sing and got a real gig—with food and girls—we figure it's time we went public." He pointed off somewhere the way rap singers do.

"Sounds like a plan," Tommy said. They did a high five.

"Don't we have to . . . you know . . . rehearse?" I asked.

"Well, like I was saying," said Albert, "we've played some together. But I suppose we should probably get in at least one practice. Or two. With you. Figure out what we're doing. How about this afternoon? We got our instruments for school band practice."

"I guess," I said.

"What kind of gig is it?" asked Tommy.

"A party. Friends of my sister."

"Cool," said Tommy. "So it wouldn't really matter what happened. Just see what goes down. We good, we're wood. If not, we rot. Skip the natter. Get to the matter."

"Right," said Albert. "We talked the talk. It's time to walk the walk. Hot to trot or we're forgot."

"Come alive or do a dive."

"Spend the dime or pay the fine."

High fives. Grins.

"Okay," I said, trying to keep up with how fast things were going.

"Got a name in mind? I mean, for the band?"

"Well, sort of," I said. "It's . . . the name is . . . Never Mind."

They grinned, nodded. "Never Mind. Cool."

"So we're set," Albert said. "Rehearse at Stuart's today. Right after school."

"Okay," I said. It was going supersonic.

"Deal?"

"Deal," I said. They held up their palms. To me too,

this time. We slapped around.

They walked off. And there I was. In a band. The Ted Runyon—Never Mind—band. As I sat there, I began to take in that we were really going to do it. With me the lead singer, and I'd never sung in my life. Not even in the shower like my dad does.

Guess what? For the rest of the day, I didn't pay attention to my classes. I was looking into the future. And the future I was looking at was not the place I wanted to go.

Never Mind?

I was minding a lot.

12.

MEG

● ○

"What's wrong?" I asked Mom as the bus pulled away. The calmness of my voice was a surprise. Inside I was freaking out.

"You tell me," said my mother. She looked grim. "And I want the truth, Margaret Beth."

Margaret Beth. My in-trouble full name. I could only nod.

"Okay. Let's go to the café," said my mother. I followed half a step behind.

The café is Café Napoli, on Broadway between 112th and 113th, where we go to have a cup of tea (Mom), a glass of milk (me), and two hard biscotti when we need to have a heavy talk. The first time she took me there was the day I cut Edward's hair for a seventh birthday present. I remember I gnawed on the harder-than-any-normal-cookie cookie and felt guilty that she was angry but, at the same time, pretty special and sophisticated.

Two years ago she brought me to the same café to talk about puberty. I took out my bite plate and tried to concentrate on the vocab—*menses, ovum*—while dipping the biscotti into my milk.

Then last year we went when my great-grandmother was

dying. Mom cried, holding her teacup, and I touched her hand across the table. Mom said, "Thank you, Meg—you love Nonni too," and I agreed, though in fact Nonni scared me. But my mother needed me to love Nonni right then, so I sort of almost managed to.

The café was for *big* moments. Yikes.

The thing is, my mother is a witch. Not nasty and cruel, though she has her moments. But what I mean is my mother knows my thoughts. She knows when I am having a problem with a friend, or when I'm feeling sad even when I am acting happy. Or, like, when I lied that time when I was like six and said I hadn't eaten any of the chocolate chip cookies. She just waited for me to admit it.

Same with what I did to Edward last year—the nose-holding onion incident. She was so angry she even fried onions a number of times to give me an opening. I had never yet admitted what I did, and she hadn't said a word. Not yet, anyway.

So I was almost relieved. I'd known for a long time this was coming, and finally, there it was. It was so like her: catch me off guard by coming home in the middle of her shift at the hospital to confront me about my cruelty to Edward.

On the way to the café, we passed a guy sitting on a blanket with a cardboard sign propped against his legs asking for food. I usually just look away, but I had my whole lunch in my bag, next to the High Achievers Club application with the blank area below community service. So I had a thought. (Or maybe I was just delaying getting to the café.)

I stopped in front of the guy, put down my bag, fished out my lunch, and offered it to him.

"What is it?" he said.

"Turkey and Swiss on rye," I told him. "Couple of Lorna Doones and a Diet Sprite."

Mom was staring at me.

The homeless man shook his head. "I'm a vegetarian," he said. "And soda is rotten for your teeth. Thanks anyway."

I took my lunch and put it back in my bag. So much for my idea of putting "Brown Bag Donations, founder" on my community service list. No, I realized. I have just been rejected by *the homeless guy*. Can I sink any lower?

Just as I got my bag rezipped, the guy said, "Actually, I'll take the Lorna Doones."

I reopened my bag. "You sure? They're cookies. Highly processed."

He shrugged, like, compromising, reluctantly.

Mom, hands on hips, said, "Margaret Beth!"

"I'm hurrying." I fished out the cookies and handed them over. I was now *founder, Cookies for the Hungry.*

My mom held the door of the café open for me. "Why didn't you eat your lunch?" She sounded suspicious.

I shrugged.

We were seated at one of the little round marble tables. My mother had refused the menus and ordered for us. "Unless . . ." She interrupted our waitress's retreat.

"Unless, Meg, do you want tea?"

Tea could stunt my growth (I could use some stunting, which is why I sneak sips of hers at home); she has never allowed me to drink tea. She thinks tall is good. Easy for petite little her to say. So why was she offering me tea? Had I grown too much even for Mom?

"Milk," I said.

Mom nodded at the waitress, then turned back to me, folding her long fingers into one another. Then she nodded at me, studying my face. My teeth started chewing on my lower lip, which was suddenly incredibly itchy. *Stay calm,* I told myself, trying desperately to remember a single relaxation exercise. *Say nothing, breathe, lower your shoulders from inside your ears. . . .*

"Who," asked Mom, "is *Ted*?"

"*Ted*?" I must have shrieked, because the waitress (Lavinia, according to her plastic name tag), who was approaching our table at that point, jumped. My milk spilled. When Lavinia tried to grab the glass, her wrist touched the hot teapot beside it. She yelped and dropped the whole tray, splattering hot water all over her cushiony brown shoes. Biscotti sailed toward the steps.

Lavinia turned and ran. At first I thought it was to get away from us. But back she came with three towels, an apology, and two busboys who helped sop up the mess while a guy (I figure he must have been the manager) yelled at them in Italian.

I lifted my feet so they could wipe under them, trying to

reorganize my head. Okay. It was about Ted. It was about making up a fake twin brother. Okay.

"Meg?" she prodded, lifting her feet so a busboy could mop beneath them.

"Ted," I said. I deserved the humiliation, but really, she was partly to blame too. She should have known from the beginning that I'd never get to be a High Achiever without deception of some sort. All that "of course you'll make it" bull. She is a doctor; she should know that if you put that much pressure on a child, she is (I am) likely to crack.

"Yes," she said, more urgently. "Ted."

"Right." *I am cracking, cracking up, right here in the café.*

She took a deep breath. "Margaret Beth, that was a very—shall I say—uncharacteristic phone message you left on the machine today."

Lavinia was walking cautiously toward us again, her tray gripped tightly in both fists.

"Message?"

Mom rolled her eyes. "Will you stop echoing my questions, please?"

"Your quest . . ." I closed my mouth. Must I be a parrot as well as a nutcase and a liar?

As Lavinia set our drinks and plate of biscotti very carefully on the table, Mom explained, "I called home to check the messages at lunchtime, and what did I hear?"

"I don't know. What did you hear?"

She glared. I looked down. *What is wrong with me?*

"I heard *you*," she said, unwrapping her tea bag and plopping it in her hot water. "Babbling about somebody named Ted. Ted, Ted, Ted, and then also a number of other boys—Rick, Joe . . . Jeremy?"

"Jeremiah," I mumbled. My crazy message from school. I forgot she sometimes calls in during the day. I slumped in my seat.

She went on, not really looking at me. "I've never heard of these boys, and what's more, you were speaking in a strange, disconnected way. Saying strange things about what they are bringing to some, well, mysterious place, sounding very nervous, very uncomfortable. Meg, are you asking for . . . help?"

"Um . . ." What is the right answer to that? I was stumped.

"Does this have something to do with why your lunch wasn't eaten?"

I shrugged. I wasn't sure. Sort of, it did, because I was such a wreck at lunch I couldn't eat. Her ESP. She'd figured the whole thing out and was way ahead of me. I nodded a little.

Mom swallowed hard. "Meg, were you . . . *smoking* something?"

"What?"

"Margaret Beth. I expect you to tell me the truth. Now."

Was I getting into trouble for smoking? The one bad thing I *haven't* been doing? I almost laughed. "Ma, I wasn't smoking anything. I wouldn't. Ever."

Mom smiled weakly and finally exhaled. Then *she* sort of laughed and covered her eyes with her hands. After a few seconds, she pulled her hands away and looked into my eyes. "Okay," she said. "I believe you."

I smiled back at her. "I really wouldn't smoke anything, Mom. Honestly. I think smoking is disgusting."

Mom poured some milk into her cup, spilling a bit. She never spills. I realized her hand was shaking. "So then," she said, "what *was* all that? I mean, who, please, *is* Ted?"

So much for relief. "Ted is . . . ," I started, reminding myself to breathe. (How gifted can a person be who has to remind herself to breathe?) "See, Edward . . ."

"Is Ted a friend of Edward's?"

"No," I said. *Did she know what was going on, or didn't she?* "He's not a . . . *friend* of . . . anybody's."

"Well, then, who is he?"

"He's . . ." I couldn't finish the sentence. How could I explain this mess I'd created? Was this just a test? Did she already know the answers and was she waiting for me to admit things? Or did she really feel as baffled as she looked?

Figuring it was safer, I tried the honesty route. "See," I began, "there's this party, Saturday night, sort of with the High Achievers Club, and Ted—he's, he was my, um—"

"Boyfriend?" she said, her voice breaking.

"Mom!" *Why does she always have to interrupt?* "No. Definitely not my boyfriend. He doesn't even . . ."

"Oh," whispered Mom, leaning close. "But you *like* him?"

She reached across the table to touch my hand. Her eyes were teary. "Oh, Meggie. I didn't even think of—"

"What are you talking about?"

"Oh, sweetheart," she sort of gushed, and Mom is not normally a gusher. More of a prober. "My little girl. Oh, my goodness. It's that . . . so you like this boy, huh?"

The probing combined with the gushing. Wonderful. Jackpot.

"Meg?"

So she really didn't know what was going on with me at all. It could be anything. It could be a *boyfriend*.

"You can tell me, Meg."

Fine, I decided. Whatever. If that's what she wants to think.

So I nodded. *Yup, sure. I like him. Why not? I invented him, didn't I?*

"Oh, Meg. And do you think he likes you too?"

I shrugged. *How could I know who he likes? He's imaginary.* I bit into a biscotti. Hard and dry as ever.

"It's very strange for me," Mom said softly, "not to know who he is, or anything about him. You're in this new school, this new program. I've always known everybody in your life, and now . . ." She sniffed and reached across the table. "Don't shut me out, sweetheart. Please. What's he like? I want to know everything about him."

13.

EDWARD

● ○

Soon as school was out, I went right to the subway station. I really wanted to get home. Maybe do some
skateboarding in the alley behind our building—
alone. Because the truth is, I had pretty much decided
that I was going to dump the whole Meg/Kimberly/
Never Mind band/stupid party thing. Drop it. Forget it.
Flip it into the can and flush it away. Never mind. No,
really never mind!

The thing is, I was sick of dueling with Meg. I needed
to leave it all alone. At least that's what the lump in the
bottom of my stomach was telling me. And when you
start getting messages from your gut bottom, it's time to
listen up.

I had made up my mind I'd call Stu when I got home
and just say, "They called the party off." Don't ask me
why I couldn't just say "forget it" to his face. Maybe
because he was always saying I didn't follow through
on my get-back plans for Meg. Or maybe it was
because he was my best friend, my only friend. Did
that mean I should always be honest with him? Or I
never should let him down? The point was, I needed

the excuse of saying someone else did it. But then, as Meg was always saying, I'm immature. Well, if I was immature, I might as well take advantage of it.

Anyway, I was just standing on the platform wishing the train would hurry up, when who should show up but Stuart, Tommy, and Albert. Tommy and Albert had their instruments with them in black cases.

"Hey, Ed," said Stuart, "where you frigging going?"

"Home."

"I thought we were going to practice."

"Today?" I said, that lump in my stomach growing to the size of a watermelon.

"The gig's on Saturday night, right?" said Albert.

"Yeah," I said.

"Well?"

"I don't know," I said. "I'm supposed . . ."

"You can call your mom from my place," said Stuart. "You told me she likes it when you come over."

"She's at work."

"So?"

"I'm not sure I can reach her."

"What about your old man?" Tommy asked.

When I didn't say anything, Stuart said, "Hey, Ed, come on, dude. This thing was your idea."

Which, being the truth, I couldn't very well say *no*, could I? But then again, as I was learning, *yes* is a seriously Super Glue word.

The express train screamed through the station on

the middle track, which gave me a few seconds off. Meanwhile Stu was giving me a lopsided look. After the train passed, he said, "You're not backing out again, are you?"

"No way," I mumbled.

The other guys were staring at me.

"Come on," Stuart pressed. "You can call from my house."

I didn't have much choice. The best I could do was haul up my backpack and follow them onto the local train when it pulled in. And I do mean follow, because the three of them were mostly talking to one another. They were going over the songs they did while I just stood there, hanging on to the pole by the door, wondering if this big hole I'd dug was going to totally swallow me.

I even started to blame Meg and that stupid High Achievers Club. Except I knew this hole was all my digging.

Stuart lives in this big apartment building on Sixty-third Street, across Broadway from Lincoln Center. His mother was there—she works at home—and she said hi, then told us to raid the food supply. While they did, I called my mother at work at her hospital.

All I got was the desk nurse assistant, Mrs. Morgan. She told me that my mother had something important come up and had left for the day.

That was unusual.

"Do you know what it was about?" I asked, worried.

"Something about your twin sister."

"Oh. If she comes back or calls in, tell her I'm at my friend Stuart's house."

"Will do, Edward."

Next I called home, but when no one answered there, I left a message that I was at Stuart's house.

Now family rule (number 262) is, when you go off somewhere unplanned, you're supposed to keep trying until you reach at least one parent. No contact, no visit. So I called Dad. He's a commercial artist, as he calls himself. He's not into commercials and he isn't artsy. What he does is design logos for some big advertising agency.

He was there.

"Hi, Dad."

"Hey, Edward. How you doing?"

"Fine," I lied.

"What's up?"

"Just wanted you to know I didn't go home. Went to Stuart's house. I couldn't reach Mom."

"His mother there?"

"Yeah."

"That's fine. Just be home for dinner."

"Okay. Bye."

"Oh, Edward!"

"What?"

"Thanks for being so responsible. You're acting

really mature. I love you."

"Love you, too," I muttered. Actually, I wished he had told me I was grounded and had to go right home immediately, because I was a bad boy. Then I wouldn't have to practice with the band.

"You okay with your folks?" Stuart said, coming to get me.

"Yeah."

"Grab something to eat. We're going up to the thirty-third floor. We can't bring food up there."

I went to the kitchen and took a piece of cake. Stuart's mom, Mrs. Barcaster, was there. I don't think I ever saw her dressed in anything but black tights— today with a hole at the right knee—a sweatshirt that read "Ski Steamboat Springs," and bare feet.

"So Edward," she said. "How's it going?"

"Fine."

"What fun. A band. Stu is really excited."

"Yeah."

"Me too. Do you think his stepdad and I could come and listen? We'd promise to keep out of the way."

"I don't know," I mumbled.

"Could you ask?" she pressed. "I think—between you and me—it would mean a lot to Stuart if we were there. This was supposed to be his weekend with his bio-father, but—as usual—he called it off. Stuart is feeling badly."

No wonder Stuart was so quick to agree to the gig.

"Yeah. Sure," I said, actually wondering, *If you dig a hole for yourself, when do you reach bottom?*

"And Edward . . ."

"What?"

"Love the band name."

"Hey, Ed!" I heard Stuart call from the front hall. "Come on! Mom, would you call Mr. Lowe and tell him we're going to be you-know-where?"

"Sure."

Walking out, I asked Stuart, "Where's 'you-know-where'?"

So Stuart, who has been my best friend since nursery school, told me, for the first time, about the thirty-third floor.

It was truly New York City weird. Seems when they built Stu's apartment building, they only had permission to build thirty two floors. Except somebody goofed, and they built thirty three. So the city said they couldn't use that floor. The result: It had to be kept empty. But that's where Stu and the guys practiced, by permission of the guy in charge of the building. Only rules: no food or drinks, and nobody can know, which is how come I never knew.

So we took the elevator up to the thirty-third floor. Stu had a key he had to turn in the elevator control panel. It was kind of creepy whooshing up there, especially when Stu made us promise that if anybody got on the elevator, we'd have to quickly push the button for thirty two and pretend we were going to the health club up there.

Nobody got on, and at the thirty-third floor the elevator doors opened to this huge place—like a cavern. Nothing but cement floor, pipes, wires. But with huge windows: You could see the Hudson River, uptown, downtown, Central Park, the roofs of the Lincoln Center buildings. New Jersey. Everywhere. What else did Stuart have going on I didn't know about?

"Wow," I said.

"This spot is the bomb, right?" said Tommy.

Stuart had his drums all set up. There was some electrical equipment there too.

"The head super, Mr. Lowe," explained Stuart, "he lives in the building. When he was a teenager, he had a band. Way back in the seventies. I guess he wanted to be a musician."

"Yeah," Tommy explained to me, "he's always telling us about his band. The Rumble Bees, or something like that. He likes to act like he's our manager."

"Is he really?" I said, impressed.

"Sort of. I mean, he knows stuff. Gives us tips. Been around," said Albert.

"And he's the one lets us use this place," said Stuart. "Gave me the key like, six months ago."

I shrugged. It was hard to look away from the windows. I could see miles. Seriously awesome.

"Yeah, Mr. Lowe is cool," said Albert.

"He knows music—way old-fashioned—Beatles stuff—but music," Tommy added.

Tommy and Albert unpacked their guitars, plugged in, and began twanging and tuning up. I was thinking, maybe if they were good, and if I didn't get in the way, it could actually work. That wouldn't be too bad. Looking out over the world like I was doing, you could sort of believe big stuff could work.

"What riffs we trying?" Stuart asked, settling in behind his drums and giving them a few whacks.

"Let's show Ed what we've been doing."

"Sure."

They settled down and then Stuart said, "One . . . two . . . one, two, three . . ." And off they went.

First of all, they were loud. I mean, *really* loud. Maybe it was just all the concrete that was there, or that the room was so big there was an echo, but I'm telling you, they were really, really loud.

Second of all, they were bad.

Bad as in no good.

Even I could tell that, though I was pretty dumb about music.

But they were fun to watch. Closing their eyes. Jumping. Strutting. Mugging. Sort of like a real band. Except they weren't. More like a takeoff of a band on some TV comedy sitcom.

Anyway, they played some, and then stopped. "Okay," Albert said to me, "what can you sing?"

That was a fun dumper right there. I mean, *sing? Me?* You might as well ask an alligator to dance. Not that I had much choice. So I named the few songs I knew.

They picked one and started to play it. I think. It was hard to tell.

"Come on," Stuart shouted over the din. "Sing!"

I felt like an idiot. Which, when you thought about it, wasn't a wrong thing to feel, because after all, I *was* an idiot.

After a while, though, I relaxed a bit and tried to remember what singers looked like—and worked on that.

The elevator dinged. The band stopped playing.

We all froze. If we were caught up there, what would happen? Stuart had said it was big trouble to be up there. We were seriously panicked, at least one of us was, though I actually thought, *If I'm in jail I won't have to go through with the party.*

Anyway, this pudgy guy came out of the elevator, looking serious. He was taller than me, but that's not saying much. He was pretty much bald save for a fuzz of hair around his ears. Round face, too, with bags under his eyes.

"Hey, Mr. Lowe," said Stuart. "What's up?"

A huge, friendly smile transformed the guy's face. "Your ma told me you guys were up here." He stuck his hands into his pockets and rocked back on his heels a bit. "How's it going?"

"Hey, Mr. Lowe, guess what? We got our first gig," said Tommy.

Mr. Lowe grinned. "A gig? Cool. Where?"

"This is my friend Edward Runyon," said Stuart. "He's our new lead singer. He got us the gig. We're playing his sister's friend's party."

"Hey, man, you got to start somewhere," said Mr. Lowe. "Be good experience. I'm all for it. The more you perform, the better you get."

"And we got ourselves a real name," said Albert.

"Which is?"

"It's . . . Never Mind."

Mr. Lowe actually laughed. "Never Mind. Love it. When's the gig?"

"Saturday night."

"*This* Saturday?" He frowned.

"Yup."

"Don't you think it's a good idea?" asked Stuart.

"Guys," said Mr. Lowe slowly, like he was trying to be careful what he said. "You know me. I'm always going to tell you the truth. No matter what. For a Saturday night gig—*this* Saturday night—what you gotta do is a whole lot of work. A *whole* lot."

That made the guys quiet.

Mr. Lowe grinned. "Hey, I'm the manager, right? I either tell it to you straight or I don't tell it."

"Sure," said Albert.

"We that bad?" asked Tommy.

"*Bad* isn't a word I like to use," said Mr. Lowe. "Know what I'm saying? How about . . . to get good, we're going to have to work real bad for it."

"That's cool," said Tommy, nodding. "I'm willing."

"Me too," said Albert.

"I'm here," said Stuart.

Mr. Lowe came over to me and shook my hand. "Carl Lowe," he said, introducing himself.

"Edward Runyon," I returned.

"Glad to have you, Ed," he said. "What do you play?"

"I . . . um . . . sing," I said. There he was being so nice but, although this whole thing started out to embarrass Meg, the one who was going to be embarrassed most was—me.

I had to do something.

14.

MEG

●○

I was sitting in the study pretending to study (really just spacing out), when Edward came in. As if my day wasn't deep enough into the toilet. Edward had to be the last person in the whole world I wanted to see.

It occurred to me to ask him when he'd spoken to Kimberly that second time but—habit mostly—I ducked behind my book so he wouldn't be able to talk to me. In that room a book is like a shield because not talking there is one of the few rules even Edward doesn't ignore. *If he talks to me*, I thought, *if he messes up the quiet of the study when I am trying to (fake) read, like he has messed up my entire life, I will truly explode at him. Yes, I will rip off his head and yell bad things down his former throat.*

When I heard what I was thinking, I couldn't believe myself. Whose thoughts are these? *Rip off his head?* I sounded like, well, like *Edward*.

I peeked over to the book to see where he was and what annoying thing he was doing because I was in the mood to let him have it. I flipped my legs down off the back of the chair and turned around, looking for him. He was sitting on the window ledge, holding a book, looking out.

Actually, he looked worried.

The world has gone inside out, I realized. Here I am having violent fantasies and getting in trouble and lying, seriously lying, to Mom and everybody else, and there's Edward, of all people, the immature and stunted weirdo, looking deep and lost in down-in-the-dumps thoughtfulness. I almost chucked my book at him.

He turned and saw me. Caught. I couldn't say, "Don't talk to me, I'm reading," because obviously I wasn't. I was staring at him. I braced myself for some asinine insult.

"Hey," he said.

"Hey yourself," I said.

He looked out the window again.

I felt bad. Guilty. I wasn't trying to be nasty. I had to say something and it just came out that way. So I quickly said, "How's your school going?"

What an original question, Meg.

He shrugged. Typical. He can't talk. But after a while he mumbled, "How's yours?"

To my annoyance I shrugged too.

"Not what you expected?" he asked.

"Well," I said quickly, not wanting him to think Fischer was too hard for me, or that I didn't belong there, which I almost definitely didn't. "It's a lot of work, of course," I said, "but I expected that. In a school like this you work—" I stopped. He just sat there. I listened to the echo of myself, like my voice was on a playback, and heard how snotty and stuck-up I sounded. And mean. I almost said, "Never mind," but changed it to "Sorry," instead.

Typically inarticulate Edward shrugged again.

"How are the kids at your school?" I asked, carefully, trying to be pleasant, interested, nonjudgmental.

"Okay," he said.

"Making any friends?" Ew. I sounded just like Mom.

He looked at me with those huge brown eyes. Right away I wanted to say I didn't mean it as an insult, or a criticism. "I mean . . ."

He lifted his chin a bit. Then he said, "Actually, yes."

"Yeah?" I said. Whoops. Worse than Mom. I sounded like an adult talking to a kid she thinks is younger than he really is. Too encouraging. Too fake. As if I was someone who should be encouraging anybody about friendships. I swallowed and said, "I'm not making any."

Edward snorted. I think it was meant to be a laugh. "How many gazillion more friends do you want? You have more friends than there are people."

"That doesn't even make sense," I snapped.

"Well, nobody ever called *me* gifted," said Edward, and picked up his book again, but since it was upside-down I was pretty sure he was only pretending to read too.

I slumped into the chair.

"Meg!" shouted Mom as she came in the front door.

"What?" I shouted back.

"Come see the new outfit I bought you for the party!"

Edward looked up from his book. "Party?"

I rolled my eyes.

He smiled.

"I'm reading!" I shouted.

Edward raised his eyebrows. It was cool. Like we were almost, maybe, friends.

"It's really cute," yelled Mom. "I bet you-know-who will really notice!"

I rolled my eyes at Edward, hoping to make him laugh.

"Who's you-know-who?" Edward asked, turning serious instead.

Right then I thought of trying to explain the whole mess to him—how there's this alternate-universe twin brother of mine named Ted, who all my new friends expect to meet at a party Saturday night. But how Mom thinks Ted is a cute boy at Fischer who is a musician and soccer player and is very smart but mostly is just a really kind boy, whom I like and who, it seems, likes me too, and, to top it off, who just might ask me out on Saturday night.

None of which was true.

Yeah, right. I could barely explain it to myself. And I was all talked out from my earlier heart-to-heart with Mom.

"Nobody," I said, thinking, *My first real boyfriend, and guess what? He's imaginary!*

"Sounds like Mom thinks it's somebody."

"Shut up," I said, and pretended to read again, thinking, even though he's not Ted, unfortunately, this mess is actually not his fault for once. It is, horrifyingly, my own. I made a list on the endpaper of my book of my current problems:

1. My hair (It always ranks number one on my what's-wrong-with-me lists; it's tradition), my five-head, my skin, my height, etc.

2. Ted is unlikely to show up Saturday (because he is imaginary; a good excuse, I have to admit).

3. Everybody in the club will discover I am a demented liar. (I don't even really like them, Annabelle and Kimberly with their application to be friends with them—still, they are the *ones*, the top, the you-have-made-it-if-you-are-friends-with-them best people in seventh grade.) They will hate me and make my life hellish.

4. Everybody else will hate me too. Even the B-list and no-list people won't let me sit with them at lunch.

5. Mom will find out everything, sooner or later, when there is no Ted to show her. I will lose the trust and respect of my parents, the one thing I've always been proudest of having.

6. Edward. (Well, he hates me already, but he's always on my list.)

7. I will be totally *alone*. (I have never been totally alone.)

8. (Left blank, but ready for my next disaster.)

"You okay?" Edward asked. I realized I was sort of starting to cry. I cleared my throat and sniffed, blinked up a few times and, when I realized I couldn't trust my voice to say "I'm fine!," gave up and shook my head.

I am so far from okay. I wished I could pour it out to somebody, a best friend, Ted. Edward?

I have made such a mess for myself and there is no way out, I actually wished I could tell him. *What should I do?* But I couldn't. He would hold it over me until our eighty-third birthday.

Edward watched me as a tear or two spilled over. It was making me crazy that I couldn't tell what he was thinking. He had every right to enjoy seeing me cry, if that's what it was. That thought made me feel more pathetic than ever.

"Anything I can do?" he asked, taking me by surprise.

Since when did he get to be the nice, generous one? That was supposed to be me.

"I wish," I said. *I really, really wish.*

He waited, sitting there, staring at me. Then I guess he gave up and stared out the window instead.

"Meg?" Mom called again from the foyer.

I was looking at Edward, at the back of his head. The back of his head is not that annoying. "Unless . . ." I forced a little laugh out. Humor is always nice at your own funeral, right? "Well, you know, if you could get a band together and by Saturday night become . . ."

"What?" His head spun toward me and he looked at me like I was insane. Which, of course, I was.

"Never mind," I said, and grunted, *his* sound, and stomped out to go see what fresh torture my mother had bought me for the big night, leaving Edward calling after me.

15.

EDWARD

● ○

"Hey, wait!" I called. "Meg!" What was that "never mind" supposed to mean?

Did she know what I was doing?

For a minute I just sat there, trying to put things together: her moodiness, her tears, something that happened to her this afternoon, her talking about the party. Most of all, Meg *does not* cry. There's a lot you can say about her—I've said it, so I know—but she *never* cries. It's a thing with her. It was pretty frustrating for a long time that, when we fought, we both knew I would be the one who'd end up in tears.

So as I sat there I thought, *What if that "emergency" that Mom left work for meant there was something seriously wrong with Meg?*

And why should I care?

It better not be something serious, I thought. *I may spend a lot of time plotting her destruction, but still . . .*

So what I did was get up and follow her out to the living room. There was my mother. She was holding up some yellow clothes in front of Meg. "It will look wonderful," Mom said, neither of them realizing that I was there.

"Ma," Meg wailed in her I-hate-my-family voice. "You don't know what you're doing!"

"Of course I do," my mother said. "It's part of the vanity of young people to think they experience everything for the first time. Trust me. I know exactly what you're going through."

"You do *not*!" Meg was in tears again. Unbelievable.

"And your young man will definitely notice," Mom added.

Young man? I thought to myself with a dozen mental exclamation points and twenty-four question marks. *What is going on?*

"Stop saying 'my young man'!" Meg screamed. The next second she turned and rushed out of the room. I could hear her slam her bedroom door behind her. Against the slamming rule. Meg crying, Meg breaking rules. Who did she think she was, me?

So I sort of just followed my mom into the kitchen. "What's the matter with Meg?" I asked, casually, I think.

"Oh, dear," my mother said. She still had the yellow clothes in her hand.

"Ahhh . . . Who's this young man you're talking about?"

My mother looked at me. Her eyes looked sad, though her mouth seemed to be on the edge of a grin. "Well," she said, "it's something about . . . Meg. But private. Which I need to respect." She shook her head. Gave a forced smile. "And how are you doing,

Edward? Any major dramas in your life?"

"Never Mind," I said. I was still trying to guess why Meg was so upset. Was it with me? The party? Something else?

"Good," Mom said, heading toward her bedroom. "Never mind sounds good to me. I mean, I thought it was hard when you were toddlers. How am I going to deal with simultaneous adolescents?"

"Don't worry, I'm immature," I said, trying to be helpful.

"Please, stay that way."

"Thanks for your support," I said. Insulted, I went down to Meg's room. Her door was closed.

I ran to my room, grabbed a book from under my bed, and snuck back to near my parents' room. As expected, Mom was already on the phone. I could tell it was Dad because she kept saying "hon." That's what she calls him.

I sat right next to the open crack of the doorway, book in hand. So what if this, in my opinion, is a good place to read? Nobody could *prove* I was spying. They should be happy I'm reading.

This is what I heard:

"Uh-huh. Uh-huh." (A lot of uh-huhs. But then . . .) "Yes, a boy. In her class, I gather, at Fischer, so he must be very bright. And you should see her face, hon, when she talks about him. There's a kind of bewilderment. Uh-huh. Uh-huh! No, she said he's very nice. No,

don't—hon, don't go all caveman on me. I know! She's my little girl too. But I—no! They haven't *kissed*. What? Because, oh, hon, calm down, I just know. She's just all excited because there's a big party Saturday with . . . Yes, a parent will be there. The girl's mother, I think. Because she said so! Oh, honey, we have no reason not to trust her. She's never given us any reason to distrust . . . Hon. Shh. Yes, a party. It's with her new classmates and she's thinking, just hoping so hard that this boy will ask her out during it. Yes, I'm sure it's perfectly . . . What? Oh, come on, honey, it's very innocent and sweet. But, hon, so . . . real."

Then she sighed for a while, I guess listening to Dad and his thoughts on the subject. Of course, nobody was going to ask me my opinion.

All I could think was that Meg was not dying. Worse: She had a boyfriend! Retch!

But actually, this *was* big news. I mean, I had always thought she hated boys. Maybe it was just me she hated.

But then, I got to thinking: *Who is this guy? Some smarty-pants, big, good-at-sports, thinks-he's-better-than-me jerk? Some guy I don't even know, and—what? He's making my sister who never cries cry?*

What did he do to her?

And why did I care? Where was *that* coming from?

It's bad enough getting older, but when it happens without my permission, it's worse.

And in fact I started to get mad, thinking, *If this jerk (her boyfriend) thinks he can mess with my sister, he has a lot to learn. I may be puny, but when I get mad, watch out.*

That settled that: If I'd had any thoughts about bagging out of that party Saturday night, they were gone. I mean, I *had* to go. Had to check out this boyfriend and let him know: You hurt one Runyon—surprise! You just bought a pain ticket from the other.

The weird thing was I meant it.

16.

MEG

● ○

I handed in my application to the High Achievers Club just before lunch, complete with my "food drives for the homeless" lie. Two Lorna Doones (one was even broken) is not a food drive. I put it on the pile facedown and turned to get away before anyone could give me a lie-detector test.

Only I bumped smack into Annabelle, who pushed me and laughed. "You're on the board of directors," she whispered. "Secretary."

Next minute Kimberly was there. "How's Ted?" she asked.

"Same," I said.

"You want to go with us to Yuki's for some sushi?" Kimberly asked. "They have half-price maki for lunch."

"Um, I told, um, somebody I would . . ."

"Oh." Kimberly shot a look at Annabelle, then smiled at me. "Okay, no problem. Maybe tomorrow?"

"Okay," I said.

"Great!" Kimberly waved as she walked backward down the hall.

I heard Annabelle saying, "I used to think she was shy."

And Kimberly answered, "Me too. She's just sure of

herself. Like a good secretary."

I sat alone at lunch. My sandwich looked gross to me anyway, so I just tossed my lunch bag into the trash (already forgetting Cookies for the Hungry) and went back to my only friend, the pay phone. I thought of calling home and leaving Mom a new message saying forget all that stuff I told you about Ted, he asked some girl named Annabelle out today, but I didn't have the energy for being consoled about my imaginary love. I toyed with my coins at the pay phone, wishing for a friend to call, until it hit me: Della.

My *real* best friend.

She'd be at school, of course, but she'd get the message after, and her voice on her answering machine at least would make me feel less lonesome.

Her voice jumped at me: "Hey, it's Della. I'm too busy to talk to you now, so leave me a message—and if you're calling about the project, leave a detailed message about your ideas. It's getting good, but we're still working, if you know what I mean. If you're calling with a bad attitude or a complaint, hang up. I don't want to hear it."

I smiled. So Della.

The beep came.

"Hey, there. It's me. Meg. It's lunch at my school and I . . . I was just, wishing we . . ."

I blinked at the ceiling. Here I was, leaving my bad attitude all over her machine. Just what she didn't want.

"I mean, I know you're not there, but . . . and I don't even know what project you're organizing. I'm sure it's good. I wish

. . . I mean I miss . . . I just don't have anybody to . . ."

Beep.

Cut off. Hung up on by her machine too. And what a stupid, pathetic message I'd left. She'd probably hear it and think, *Uh-huh. I was right. I told Meg not to leave us for that ego-trip smarty-pants school, and now she's all alone, stuck with a bunch of high-on-themselves snorkly losers. Serves her right for turning her back on her real friends. Good-bye.*

Maybe Della wouldn't think all that, I told myself. Maybe she didn't hate me, though she hadn't called me since Monday, when we talked for about an hour, and neither had anybody else from my old school. Maybe they were just all busy with their projects, their lives, like I'd been busy with my sorry mess of a life. I mean, I hadn't called her, either. And it was really only one night, since Della won't talk on the phone on Tuesdays (all her favorite shows are on).

But still.

I hung around the pay phone until lunch was over. In fact, I sort of wandered through the rest of the day, and then, when I got home, I checked my e-mail. There was one from Della:

Nut-Meg:
What's up? Nut-ball message. Call me.
Della

I e-mailed her back:

Della –

My life is so

But I couldn't finish because just then Dad came in. As if my life weren't messed up enough.

I hit Send to get the e-mail off my screen, then signed off.

When I turned around, Dad was just looking at me and nodding—like a bobble-head. Bad sign. I grabbed my journal, just for something to hold.

"Hi," I said.

He kept nodding, but said, "Hi."

I sat down in my book nook, because it was the closest thing I had to the cave I wished I could crawl into. My behind hurt. I was sitting on a pencil, it turned out. I yanked it out from under me and started chewing on it.

"So . . . ," Dad said. "May I sit down?"

"Ah . . . sure." I bit the eraser off the pencil. But then what? To swallow it would be gross. So would spitting it out.

He sat down in my desk chair. "Meg," he said, swiveling around. I could tell it was going to be a doozy right away by the way he kept clearing his throat. He picked up a plastic Wizard of Oz Scarecrow from my desk and started twirling it on its base.

"What's up, Dad?" I was choking on tiny bits of rubber from the gnawed-up eraser. I wasn't even sure it was rubber.

"We have to talk."

I wiped my tongue casually on my sleeve and then, in my journal, I used the pencil to write, *Uh-oh.*

"So," he said, trying to sound casual while wringing the Scarecrow's neck. "How's school?"

"Fine," I said. I underlined the *uh-oh*. My mouth tasted like an old bird's nest. The idea that my tongue could double as an eraser was interesting—useful.

He said, "The work's not too hard?"

I shook my head.

"And the kids? How are you finding them?"

"All right there in the classroom when I walk in," I said.

Dad laughed. "I meant . . ."

"I know," I said. "They're okay."

"Yeah?"

"I guess," I said. "A couple of real zip drives, some nice ones." I wrote, *What does he really want to know?*

"How about that High Achievers Club? How's that coming?"

I shrugged. "Fine, I guess. I don't know. Maybe you were right about it."

"Really?" he asked. "What did I say?"

"You know, why would I want so badly to be in with a bunch of snotty . . ."

"Are they?"

"No, actually," I said, choking a bit on some leftover eraser crumbs. "They're . . . nice."

"So then . . ."

"Never mind. I mean, forget it." I cleared my throat.

He cleared his throat again too. "I hear there's a party you want to go to this Saturday night."

"Yeah," I said. "Why? Do we have other plans? Are we

planning a family trip or something?" I wrote, *Please! Say we have to be someplace else! Rescue me! (Family rule 101—family comes first; rule 101a—when I want it to.)*

"No," he unfortunately said. "But, um . . ."

"What?"

"Mom is under the im . . . or she thinks, well, she told me about, that you were feeling, you know . . ." He was twisting the Scarecrow faster and faster on its base.

I wrote, *She told him!*

"The . . . this boy," he said. "In your class. Who you, well . . . and I had this idea. Or question. Or maybe actually it is more of a suggestion."

I hid my head in my hands. My father was about to give me advice about a boy. *Oh, gag.* Was he about to tell me how to kiss or something? *Please, God, no.* I absolutely could not handle hearing from my father about boys. But there he was, blushing and torturing my Scarecrow, thinking I was hooking up with some hottie in my class. *Oh, dear God, kill me now.* Or maybe he didn't want to tell me how to kiss, which oh, man, would be horrible enough— but no, maybe he was actually totally freaking out about his little girl getting involved with this boy; and me, of all people—huge, dorky, unwantable, uninterested-in-boys *me*—was about to get into all kinds of trouble with my father over this potential boyfriend that *I had completely invented*!!!!!

He twisted my Scarecrow so much its head popped off. He gasped. "Oh, Meggie, I'm sorry!"

He started shoving the Scarecrow head onto the spindle neck part so hard I thought he might pulverize the whole thing.

"Dad! Stop!"

He looked down at his hands and turned bright red. He dropped the pieces on my desk and turned the chair away from me to stare out the window.

"Sorry," he mumbled.

"It's okay."

He shook his head. "I'm not very good at this," he said.

At that exact moment I decided, *I have to tell him. I am going to tell him the truth and whatever the consequences are, so be it; maybe he'll help me figure out some damage control.*

"Dad . . . ," I started.

He turned, held up his hand, and smiled at me, this really fake smile, and said, "I was thinking, what about if you invite him over to play Monopoly?"

"Who?"

"The . . . the boy, Meg. In your class. Who you like. That would be nice. We could all meet."

"Play . . . *Monopoly*?"

"Sure. We'd give him first pick of tokens. Even my favorite, the shoe. Unless you want to give him yours: the Scottie, right? You still like that one, right?"

"Dad . . . there is no boy."

"That would be nice, wouldn't it? We could get to know him. He could get to know us. Token choice reveals a lot."

"Dad, no, seriously. There is *no* boy. I made the whole thing up."

There. I said it.

Dad stared into my eyes for a few seconds before I had to look at the floor. Admitting the truth is a relief, but at the same time it sucked. My whole body was shaking.

"Meg . . ." He sounded disappointed.

I closed my eyes, knowing I deserved whatever he was going to say.

He said, "You don't have to hide the truth. It's perfectly natural what's happening. Mom already told me about him."

"No, Dad," I said. "Seriously. I made the whole thing up. Ted does *not* exist."

"Oh, yeah, Ted," said Dad. "I apologize for forgetting his name."

"Dad," I cried, "you're *not* getting it."

He stood up, slipped his hands into his pockets, and sort of rocked there for a minute. "I'm not trying to make a big deal about this, Meg. I'm just suggesting . . . a game of Monopoly. If you want to suggest another game . . . Scrabble is fine too. But boys don't generally spell well. Maybe he does; you don't want to generalize. Hey, what about Hearts? In college I loved playing Hearts. Guys love cards. For low stakes, of course. Say . . . a penny a point. Or . . . toothpicks."

"Toothpicks?"

"Or M&M's. That could be fun."

"Dad," I said. "Listen to me: There—is—no—Ted."

"What I would like," he went right on, "and your mom feels the same way—that it would be nice, if . . . you and Edward know that your friends are always welcome here."

"Yes, but . . ."

"And Monopoly really is a good game. A family classic. We have that deluxe set we haven't taken out in so long. . . ."

I opened my mouth but couldn't figure out where to begin again.

"Right?" he asked, sounding like pleading. "You know, the nice *deluxe* set? Tin box. The swivel?"

I nodded. It was no use. He had his thing he needed to tell me, and nothing I could say was getting through to him. We have the deluxe set, so everything will be fine.

He cleared his throat. "Okay?"

I nodded. Lying again. I was so far from okay.

More rocking, more throat clearing. "I guess you probably, well, your mom is the . . . But there is no reason we can't have open lines of communication, you and I. That's the key, Meg. Honesty. Father and daughter. We can . . . talk. Father. Daughter. Communicate. Right? That's all I'm trying to say. I don't like it that you feel you have to hide this. Of course, this is a milestone, or rite of passage, as it were, but . . ."

"Dad . . ."

He strode over to my door, gripped the doorknob, and took a deep breath, then yelled, "I want this boy to come play Monopoly!"

"He can't!" I shouted.

"Why?"

"He is imaginary!"

"I will not be lied to!" he yelled back, and slammed my door on his way out. Two seconds later the door creaked open slightly. Dad mumbled, "Sorry. We could, I mean, I could buy some new crisp money. Might impress him." He left again.

I stared at my almost-closed door for a while. I wished I had someone to help me figure out what had just happened and what to do about it all. I needed to talk to someone who would listen, really listen, and who knew me and cared about me and was smart and could really set me straight.

Della.

I logged back on to my e-mail.

Della had written back:

So what?

So what? I pour out my guts and she just disses me? I couldn't remember how far I'd gotten into telling her what was going on, but she was supposed to be my best friend. So what? I don't think she's ever said anything so mean to me in her life. I couldn't believe she would be like that.

I knew I had to call her immediately, or I'd never be able to forgive her.

17.

EDWARD

● ○

There was a knock on my bedroom door.

"Yeah?"

"Telephone," came my dad's voice, a bit strained. "For you."

"Who is it?" I asked, since my incoming calls are about one a month—maybe.

"I don't know. Not Stuart."

Puzzled—no one called me except Stu—I got up and went into the kitchen to get the phone. Just before I picked it up, I turned around. Meg was there.

"Is that for me?" she demanded.

I said, "No, me."

"Who is it?"

"One of my friends you don't know."

She said, "Tell Stuart to make it quick. I have to call Della."

When she just stood there, I said, "Excuse me. My phone calls are private."

"Oh my God!" she screamed. "Everything is going crazy!" She stomped off somewhere.

I picked up the phone. "Hello?"

"Is this Edward . . . I mean Ted?" It was Kimberly. The elf whisperer.

"Yeah."

"Hi."

"Hi," I said, feeling like I was bungee diving without the bunge.

"I wanted to talk to you about the party."

"Oh."

"I mean your band and all. Never Mind. Such a cool name. Oh, guess what? I think I heard one of your songs on the radio just now. I was doing homework. Not really paying attention. I think the DJ said it was you. On LIR. I'm pretty sure I heard him say Never Mind."

I couldn't say anything. I wanted to point out the obvious, that the DJ couldn't have possibly played anything by us. We didn't exist. But I just couldn't. Not that it mattered. She went right on.

"I just want to make sure we've got everything all right. The way you would like. "

I sighed. "Okay."

"I'm afraid our living room isn't huge, really, and the furniture is, well . . . my mom didn't want to chance that anybody would, well, anyway, they said we could move some into the dining room and some into the family room. Does that sound okay?"

Why should I care what she does with her furniture? "I guess."

"Okay," she whispered. "Great. So you guys can set up at one end and we can dance at the other. It'll be like an . . . intimate . . . dance floor. Is that okay?"

"Sure."

"And I just had to tell you—*so* many people want to come. I mean, this is going to be the best, coolest party ever. I mean, it's just about the biggest thing of the year. So I really appreciate it."

"Sure."

"And there's another thing. . . . I hope you don't mind."

"What?"

"There's this boy at Fischer. His name is Phelps."

"Phelps?"

"I think it's a family name. That's what my mother says. Meg knows him. Phelps Bartlebye. Really cute. Anyway, he heard about the party. And guess what? His father is in the record business. I mean he works for it. The company is called Rolling Rock Records. . . ."

"Oh." New question: Do sinking feelings ever stop sinking?

"Is it big?" she asked.

"I guess," I said, never having heard of it, but still sinking.

"Oh, wow. Anyway, Phelps heard about the party. I really don't know how. And he said, if I invited *him* to the party, he would bring along his *father*! So he could hear you guys play! Is that not too cool? I'm only doing it, I thought, you know—for you. Is that okay?"

"I guess. . . ."

"So he'll be here too. If he, you know, like, discovered you at . . . my party . . . wouldn't it be amazing?"

"Yeah. Amazing."

"Except—I'm *so* dumb—you've already been discovered. Right?"

"I'm afraid so."

"Um, Ted? Can I ask you something . . . personal?"

"Yeah."

"I wanted to know . . . like . . . you know . . . if . . . well . . . Do you have a girlfriend?"

"A girlfriend?"

"If you have one, I mean, you could bring her. Do you?"

"Not exactly."

"Oh, wow."

"Yeah."

"Well," she said after a moment, "I . . . don't have a boyfriend."

"Oh."

"Did Meg tell you about me?"

"A bit."

"Well . . . she told me a lot about you."

"She did?"

"You know how some brothers and sisters—even twins—how they don't normally get along?"

"Yeah."

"Well, you should know, your twin sister is *not* like that. She thinks you are absolutely the greatest. She adores you."

"She does?"

"Well, all she does is talk about you."

"Oh."

"Honest. She's *so* proud of you. Which I think says a lot about you—I mean, if your own sister likes you. My kid sister, Brett, hates me. For no reason. Anyway, I don't know why I just told you that."

"Me either," I said.

She laughed. "You are so funny. And *so* easy to talk to. It's like, we have a connection. You know?"

"Uh-huh." Right. A connection. Sure.

"It's kind of amazing, isn't it?" she asked.

"I guess."

"Do you like shy girls?"

"No," I said. Because actually I don't like any kind of girls. I think.

"Good," said Kimberly. "I knew you wouldn't. I could tell. And I'm not a shy girl."

"Okay," I said.

"So here's my big question," she said. Big pause. Breathing. "Ummm . . . will you go out with me?"

"Huh?"

"What?"

"I didn't say anything," I said.

"Oh, I thought you, sounded sort of, shocked, or,

109

never mind. Ha! Never Mind. So cool. Because I was thinking that way, if Meg had a boyfriend . . ."

"She does."

"She does?"

"Yeah."

"Oh, wow! Is it Phelps? I thought I saw them together before Math today."

My mind started going a million miles an hour, working on this guy, Phelps. That must be *him,* Meg's "young man." Some rich jerk, thinking his father is some big-shot music guy and that gave him the right to upset my sister. I would rip his head off and curse down his (former) throat. "Yeah," I said. "Phelps." Saying his name felt like spitting.

And I was thinking also, *Why should I worry about Meg?* when I realized Kimberly was saying, "Because then we could, like, double-date."

"Oh, yeah," I said sarcastically. Like, *no way.*

"So—is that a *yes*?"

I had stopped paying attention to Dimberly and was plotting violent revenge on this bat-ding Phelps, while wondering again why he should bother me. So I said what I say to my mom when she's waiting for an answer and I have no idea what she's been babbling about: "Um, yeah . . ."

I was so mad I was pacing. This Phelps was planning to show up at the party thinking he could mess with my sister and then pass judgment on me? I was so

110

sick of people judging me!

"Great. Wow," she went on without hearing a word of what I was thinking. "I've been telling my mom *all* about you, and she's the one who encouraged me to ask you out, stop waiting for you to make the moves. You know? And she was right. She's a feminist."

"Oh," I said, trying to catch up by thinking, *Who*? Is a *what*?

"Okay, so anyway, see you Saturday, then, Ted. Or would you rather I call you Edward, like your family does?"

"Whatever."

"Okay. Bye, um, boyfriend!" And she hung up.

Huh? What just happened? Boyfriend?!

I stood there, holding on to the phone, trying to go through everything that she had said. It was a little weird. No, it was a lot weird. There was her party: She had taken the furniture out of the living room. Then there was this guy—Phelps—bringing his father from a record company to discover my stinking band, who my sister either loved or hated but who was obviously leftover cow pie. Somebody was a feminist. And, worst of all, Dimberly was supposed to be my—girlfriend?

I tried it in my head again a few times, wanting to make sure I got it straight. Except, of course, it wasn't straight at all. It was a double-twisted pretzel. I needed some help.

I went looking for my father.

He was in the study reading a paperback book. I could see the title:

RAISING TEENAGERS
When Hormones Take Over the Home

"Dad," I said, "can I talk to you?"

He put down the book right away—guiltylike, and looked at me. "Let me guess," he said. "You've got a girlfriend."

I gasped. "How did you know that?"

"I'm learning fast," he said, holding up the book. "Perhaps, at least, you can tell me about her."

"Her name is, well . . . Kimberly."

"Okay. Nice. Can . . . you describe her?"

"Dad. That's the whole thing. . . . I've . . . I've never even *met* her."

He looked at me sort of funny. "Your girlfriend. And you never . . . *met* her?"

"No way."

He hitched forward in his chair. "Edward, can I ask you something?"

"Yeah."

"Is she . . . *imaginary*?"

"Imaginary?" I cried. "I wish!"

"You do? Why?"

"Because I don't want a girlfriend."

"But still, you . . . have one?"

"Yeah. And she's too real for me."

He sat back. "That's a relief. I suppose if you have to choose between an imaginary friend that you really want and a real friend you don't want, I'd say you're in pretty good shape."

"What are you talking about?" I asked.

He held up a hand to keep me from talking. "Wait. I have just one question to ask," he said.

"Yeah? What?"

"Does she play Monopoly?"

"Forget it!" I yelled. "Why can't anyone ever take me seriously?"

"What's her favorite token?" I heard him ask.

I stormed out and went toward my room. But as I went past Meg's door, I couldn't keep myself from opening it and sticking my head in. She was doing homework.

"I happen to know who your jerky boyfriend is."

She looked up, startled. "What are you talking about?"

"Not what. *Who*. And the answer is Phelps."

I slammed her door and then my own.

18.

MEG

● ○

Phelps?

Why would Edward think I had a boyfriend at all? Unless—oh my God—Mom told him, too. But that couldn't be, because she thought my boyfriend was *Ted*. So why would he think *Phelps*? Phelps, who is only the cutest seventh grader at Fischer. Phelps, who I am sure has no idea who I am. The distance, socially, from Phelps to me had to be like the distance from Kimberly to, well, Edward. Who Kimberly thought she was falling in love with just from my description. But no, wait: It was Ted she loved. My boyfriend, my brother. My head was spinning.

All I could think about was that real life had ended and the freaky inside-out wacko-world had taken over. Me and Phelps and Kimberly and Ted—maybe we could all go out together sometime soon. Maybe to the movies, and pizza afterward, and the couples would hold hands and oh, my aching head, I am really bonkers now.

I wandered down the hall and called Della.

"Hello?"

"Hey there," I said, but quietly, cool, like Kimberly.

"Hello?" Della repeated. "Hello?"

"Hello," I managed to get out, but she was yelling.

"If you're trying to sell something, we're not buying," Della said, and hung up. I hung up too and slunk back to my room.

I flopped down on my bed and buried myself under the covers, fully dressed, with my head under all my pillows including decorative. Maybe I would wake up soon and, like in the stories I used to write in elementary school, all this would have been a dream.

The problem was—I wasn't sleeping.

I wouldn't have faked sleep if Mom had said it was Della on the phone a few minutes later. I snuck to my door and listened to Mom talking to *my* best friend, thank you: "Oh, she's been so busy she just conked out, I guess, but I'm sure she'll call you tomorrow." She lowered her voice. "Della, has she told you about her new boyfriend?"

Oh, great. Just dandy.

19.

MEG

● ○

I woke up hearing Edward faking a stomachache. At least some things hadn't changed.

I tried on six different shirts and four different pants, gave up, and wrote myself a note:

1. Find a style.
2. Buy some new clothes (*not* yellow).
3. Try to look more Kimberly (maybe if my name were an adverb? Megly?).

I left on my not-too-disfiguring black pants and short white sweater. Boring but inoffensive, I decided. I put new makeup over my old makeup. Disgusting, but not as disgusting as I would be without the mask of it. *There*, I thought. *New day, new me.*

I wish.

Just a dream, I doodled in my notebook on the way to school.

Oh, I really, really wish.

You would think this stupid party was the Academy Awards.

At school nobody could sit still, nobody could stop talking about it—how Never Mind was going to play, and the
lead guy, my twin, Ted, was supposedly *going out with
Kimberly. What?* She actually called me her sister-in-law.
What!?

The major buzz was over which people Kimberly was
going to allow to come and which she was not, because
apparently there were many kids still on the maybe-list, all
pathetically trying to suck up to her. An invitation meant you
were *in* the High Achievers Club and a dis meant you were
out, a nobody.

I, of course, made the cut. No problem. Being Ted's sister and all.

I was shockingly popular. It made me feel sick.

Everybody wanted to know what I was going to wear. When
I said I had no idea, they all nodded like I was cooler than
cool. When I said that my mother had bought me a horrifying
bright yellow outfit, four girls in my social studies class
laughed their heads off.

I was comedy queen for the day.

Two seventh graders I didn't really know asked if I could
possibly get them invited and offered to do "anything" for
me in return. Feeling giddy, I said, "I invite you," but when
they became ecstatic, I regretted the joke. Only it was too
late.

The four laughing girls from social studies sat with me at
lunch, asking me more about the yellow outfit, cracking up
at every word I uttered.

Walking down the hall to English, Annabelle and Kimberly flanked me. Kimberly had her arm linked through mine while Annabelle pumped me for information on the other guys in the band and which ones I thought had girlfriends.

I promised her I would try to find out.

Even weirder, everybody wanted to know what was going on with me and Phelps. Me and Phelps? *Nothing*, I kept saying. Nobody believed me. The more I asked, "Who told you about me and Phelps?" the more it sounded like there really *was* a "me and Phelps." When I told the truth, they were sure I was lying, but my lies had become the foundation of the world.

As Kimberly and Annabelle and I strolled in from the pizza place after lunch (Kimberly insisted on paying for mine, and laid out a twenty on the counter), Kimberly elbowed me hard in the side.

"What?" I turned to glare at her, but she stopped walking so I ended up glaring right into the bluest eyes I have ever seen.

Phelps.

"Uh," I said charmingly. I checked my teeth with my tongue for stray bits of cheese, I hope unobtrusively.

"Hey," he said, and then smiled.

I stopped walking because my legs had stopped functioning.

"See you tomorrow night," he said, and continued down the hall.

My new best friends Kimberly and Annabelle grabbed me.

I have no idea what they were saying. They just talked and talked, high-pitched chatter, *lucky, wearing, cute, excited*— I don't know. I plunked down in my seat and waited for Science to start.

Ms. Holmes wrote SCIENCE FAIR! on the board and told us that for our projects this year there would be assigned partners. Row one with row two, row three with row four, the person beside you, no switching, get started on brainstorming what your project will be.

I heard Kimberly, row two, front, and Annabelle, row three, front, both going "Aw!" Kimberly turned and gave me the most pouty face I'd ever seen, like she was so heartbroken not to be with me. I, practically her sister-in-law, shrugged back.

I looked to my left to see who my partner was. I have to admit I was just hoping it wasn't one of those annoying High Achievers.

It wasn't. It was Esther Grossbart.

She looked at me and grimaced. I, turns out, was one of those annoying High Achievers.

I dragged my desk over to hers.

The two of us just sat there like dumb cows for a while as the rest of the class partnerships jabbered excitedly.

My mind was a total blank. Science? When life was in chaos?

Hey, maybe we could create a clone (of my imagination) called Ted who would actually show up at—never mind. Ugh!

I turned to Esther. Her gaze was steady and her mouth was straight. It was obvious she was wondering why she had to get stuck with me as a partner. I figured I might as well let her get it off her chest, so I said, "Well, what?"

"I'm interested in atomic structure," she said.

"Huh?" I replied, brilliantly.

"I was thinking maybe we could make a model of an atom."

"For the science fair?" I asked.

"No," she said. "Just for kicks."

We stared at each other. Then one side of her mouth stretched a tiny bit, and turned up, into what, a smirk? A smile? I felt my mouth doing the same.

"Sounds like a kick," I said back.

She blinked, twice, then looked down to her notebook.

"Actually," I said. "A model atom sounds like a really good idea."

"I was thinking we could cut open balls. Those little pink balls, what are they called?"

"My dad calls them Spaldeens," I said.

"Mine too," said Esther. "I was thinking we could use one of them to hold the nucleus."

"We could make the protons and neutrons out of golf balls," I suggested. "Or M&M's."

"Yeah," said Esther. "Perfect! With the different colors representing the different—"

"Yeah," I said. "And then for the electrons we could. like, rig something up with wire or—"

"Yeah," said Esther. "And we could use, maybe, Jelly Bellies for the electrons, so it wouldn't droop from the weight of—"

"Yeah," I said. "Talk about a heavy-metal atom." She didn't interrupt, didn't say anything. I wished I could suck that sentence back in. What a dorky joke.

But Esther smiled. "I like that," she said.

We both looked down at our notebooks.

"We should choose which atom," she said.

"Okay," I agreed. "What's your favorite?"

She grinned. "Cookie dough dynamo."

I said, "How about chocolate chip mint?"

"Anything but carbon or oxygen."

"You got something against air?" I asked, not just to prove I knew what that meant. Well, maybe. It's scary how insecure I am.

"Nothing personal against it," she said. "I was just thinking it would be good to do something complicated. If that's okay with you."

"Don't worry," I told her. "I am the queen of complicated." And I thought, *That has to be the most true thing I've said since I started seventh grade.*

"Me too," said Esther.

"Really?" I was suddenly curious about her.

"I think it's the age," she answered.

I couldn't tell if she meant the age we are or the age we live in, and I didn't get a chance to ask because it was time to move our desks back and put our books on the floor for a pop quiz on the chapter we were supposed to have studied last night.

I had completely forgotten to study.

I got ready for my normal stress attack: the sweating, shaking, heart-thumping way I always feel when I know I am about to be exposed for the fraud I am. I went through the check points from chapter one of my stress-reduction book and, when I got to my face (step one), I realized I was smiling.

Smiling?

Maybe it was the relief of having had a normal conversation for the first time in a while. For a few minutes there, my life felt acutely ordinary. It was just school, just atoms, just working on a project and going back and forth about ideas with somebody smart, funny, nice. It felt really good.

When I glanced over there, Esther looked pretty happy too. Though probably that's because she was prepared for the quiz. And on this quiz it wouldn't matter how cool you were.

You gotta love a quiz like that.

But I had to hate the fact that the party was only about thirty hours away.

20.

EDWARD

● ○

I tried to stay home from school, but my parents would not believe me about whatever I was saying was wrong, health-wise. So unfair. I did the next best thing. As Dad and I sat on the crowded subway, I sulked.

"Something bothering you?" my father asked halfway there.

"I don't feel good."

"Edward, it has been shown, statistically, that two out of three school days you announce that you are not feeling well. Likewise, it has been shown, statistically, that, without fail, on days when you do *not* have to go to school you never complain about your physical condition. What can we learn from this?"

"Sleeping late improves my health."

He actually laughed. "But seriously, what's up?"

"Never Mind," I said.

"That's not very helpful."

"It's the truth," I said, not wanting to explain that I was actually telling the truth.

"Have plans for the weekend?"

"Hang out with Stuart."

"Our place or his?"

"Why?"

"Because on Saturday night I gather your sister has a party to go to. She's all excited—or rather tense—about it."

"Oh?"

"Seems she has a . . . boyfriend." He gave me a quick glance. "Did you know anything about that?"

"Sort of."

"Know anything about him?"

"Never Mind."

"Edward, I'm trying to have a serious talk."

I sighed.

"But, if 'never mind' is the way you feel about it, well, then, so be it: Never mind. What I was about to tell you, however, is that your mother and I will be dropping in at her party. At least that's the plan. Meg knows we're bringing her, of course, and maybe that we're planning to just, you know, step in, but then we might, kind of, linger. For a while."

No way! That meant they would see me in the band too! My whole life was going to end at that stupid party!

My father, not knowing my thoughts, or that I had just died a few times, chatted on. Made me think that sure, parents want you to grow up and live, but they don't seem to notice how often you die.

"We don't know the family of the girl who's having this party," he went on, paying no attention to my thoughts, "and we just think it's a good thing to check things out, make sure. And also to show that, well, that our family is involved. But I don't want to leave you all alone. . . ."

"I'll be with Stuart."

"Great."

I spent the rest of the ride wondering whether or not I should tell Meg that our parents were going to be at this party. By the time we got to Thirty-fourth Street, I still hadn't made up my mind.

"See you at dinner," my father said as he got out. "Love you," he added.

By the time I wandered into school, I had made up my mind: I was *not* going to the party. One way or another I would *not* show up. My parents were going. Let them deal with Phelps.

Stuart was at the front door of school, waiting for me.

"What's up?" I said.

"The word is out."

"What word is out of what?" I asked.

"People know about the party. And our—you know—Never Mind playing there."

I sighed. "How'd that happen?"

"I think Tommy and Albert were talking. . . ."

I must have had some look on my face because

Stuart said, "Come on, it's not *supposed* to be a secret, is it? We want people to know about us."

"I guess," I mumbled.

"So people here at school know, and now they want to come too."

I don't know if I actually turned green, but I *felt* green. "How many?"

"No idea. Is that a problem? You said Kimberly was rich."

"Whatever," I said. "Better get to class."

That day, maybe twenty dozen times people came up to me—I didn't even know most of them—and asked me about the party, and where it was, and could they come. Considering I didn't know the answers to any of those questions, I handled myself pretty well. That is, I kept saying, "Sure. Cool," or words like that. After a while I almost enjoyed doing it. I mean, tons of people suddenly knew me. No one held their nose. I was never so popular in my life. I told myself to enjoy it— five hours of popularity—'cause when I didn't show up at the party, all that would end.

After school I called home and left a message that I was at Stu's house and was staying for dinner. When we got to the rehearsal room, the first thing that Tommy said to me was, "Hey, dude, we don't even know where this gig is, or when."

"I don't know either," I said.

They looked at me as if I were stupid which, no

coincidence, was the way I felt. So I sighed and said, "I can find out."

"I got a cell phone," Albert said. It was in my hand before I could do or say anything. I dialed Kimberly's number, praying she wouldn't be home.

"Hello?" she whispered.

"Kimberly?"

"Ted?"

"Uh . . . yeah."

"Oh, wow. I was just thinking about you."

I did not know what to say to that, and the guys were all watching me. I turned my back to them and just stood there.

"How are you?" she whispered.

"Fine," I lied.

"Getting psyched for the party?"

"I don't have your address."

"Oh! I'm so stupid! Ten-forty-five Park Avenue. Apartment twelve-E."

I repeated it out loud while Tommy wrote it down.

Kimberly, meanwhile, continued in a mad rush. "And Ted? Can you come at seven o'clock? I mean, the party is supposed to start at eight, but you'll want to get here early and set up. Right? And, you know, you and me, get together. Talk. Meet, really. Isn't it *weird* we've never met face-to-face, yet?"

"Yeah, weird," I agreed.

Stuart punched me in the back.

"I gotta go rehearse," I said.

"Oh, wow. You're calling me from band practice?"

"Yeah."

"Wow," she said again. "Ted?"

"Yeah?"

"One thing: Did you tell Meg I asked you out?"

"Why?"

"Well, I just, this is stupid, but—and unfeminist, I know—but I sort of lied about something. Don't be mad."

"Okay," I said.

"I told everybody *you* asked *me* out."

"Oh."

"Are you mad?"

"No. Just . . . insane."

She laughed. "You are so . . . cute!" she said.

The guys were all shoving me by now, and Albert was grumbling something about his cell-phone minutes.

"I really gotta go," I said

"Okay," whispered Dimberly. "Oh, and Ted?"

"Yeah?"

"People don't know we haven't met. It's like you said, too insane. People wouldn't get it. You know? How people are? Shallow people? So you do look like Meg, right? Only, a boy. And much taller than she is, right?"

"Uh . . . right," I said.

"Good. Because I'm a little taller than she is, so . . ."

"See ya." I hung up, visions of a stork and a frog in my head.

The guys were all looking at me.

"What about transportation?" said Tommy. "All this stuff."

There was no time to answer. Mr. Lowe showed up. "Hey guys," he said. "The gig still on?"

"It's on," said Stuart.

"Great," said Mr. Lowe. "But this is no time to be just standing around talking, okay? Now, some important questions: What kind of audience do you think you'll have? A performing artist must always think of the audience. You're not there alone. You are performing *for* them, with them. So, what do we got, just kids?"

They all looked at me again.

"It'll be mostly kids," I said. Then, remembering, I said, "Plus a few adults, I guess."

"Parents?" asked Mr. Lowe. "If so, we need to be extra careful about language. I mean, you need to be cool. You want other gigs to come out of this, right? Sure you do. So," he said, looking at me, "some parents and . . . ?"

"Well, one of the parents is from a record company."

"No way," said Tommy.

"You never told us that," said Stuart.

"Hey," said Mr. Lowe. "Let's let Edward explain."

"Well, just that, one of the kids, his father works for a record company."

"Which one?" asked Albert.

"Ah . . . Rolling Records . . . Something like that. "

"Triple R? Rolling *Rock* Records?" said Mr. Lowe.

"That's it."

"You're kidding," he said.

"No. It's true."

"What's the guy's name?"

"Whose name?" Phelps, I was thinking. Phelps.

"The parent with the record company."

"I don't know . . . Bartle. . . something."

"Bartlebye? *Jason* Bartlebye?"

"I don't know his first name." Just his kid, Phelps. Who makes my sister cry.

"Jason Bartlebye is coming to hear you guys? "

"Do you know him?" asked Albert.

"Know him? Jason Bartlebye is one serious big music honcho. You sure? Jason Bartlebye is really going to be there?"

"Is that bad?"

"Gentlemen," said Mr. Lowe in a whole different voice, "I don't want to put the pressure on, but you're getting the chance of a lifetime. This is real. This is big time. This is serious. I think we had better get ourselves into some real work."

As for transportation, Mr. Lowe said he'd take us in his van. "No way I'm going to miss this," he said.

I didn't get home till about nine that night.

When I got there, I checked in with my folks, did the usual quick "Did you have a nice time at Stuart's?— Yeah" bit, then went to my room. Right away a knock came on my door. "It's me, Meg. I have to talk to you."

"Forget it," I said. I didn't even want to look at her. This Phelps guy would never be threatened by puny me. There wasn't much I could do to help Meg, I had to admit. It was no use imagining that my going to this party would fix anything.

I heard her retreat down the hallway.

Ten minutes later, another knock.

"I'd like to talk to you." My mother.

"I'm too tired," I said, turning off my light.

She too retreated.

A third knock.

"Edward." It was my father. "I want to continue our conversation from this morning."

That time I pretended to be asleep. He poked his head in, saw the light out, and went away. I heard him say something to Mom about me and Meg both sleeping more than usual, and did she think we might have mono?

Mom said, "Kids often express depression with excessive sleep. They couldn't be depressed, could they? Things are going so well for both of them."

Actually, I was sleeping less than ever. But then the party was less than twenty hours away.

21.

EDWARD

● ○

I used to love Saturdays. But when I woke up, I wished it was Monday and I had to go to school. But no, it was Performance Day.

I lay in bed for a while, trying to think of the whole situation as a computer game. But if it was a computer game, I would do what I always did, find the cheat codes that let me win.

So I tried to imagine what the cheat codes would be for this game.

A force field that would make me look like anybody except who I really was.

A double force field to make people think I was cool.

A musical talent that would let me sing so well that everybody would swoon into a faint.

A pair of shoes that would make me a foot and a half taller and again as wide.

Brains.

Trouble was, my real life didn't have a cheat code.

And, since Mr. Lowe insisted that we rehearse all day—starting at nine A.M., I got up.

I sat down to a breakfast of French toast with my folks.

"Where's Meg?" I asked.

"Still in bed," my dad said from behind his part of the newspaper.

"What are your plans for today?" my mother asked from behind her part of the newspaper.

Yeah, good question. But I mumbled, "Going to Stuart's."

"Again? All day?"

"Tonight, too."

"Oh, well, fine," she said. "Just keep us informed."

They didn't even care!

Once again I felt this urge to blurt the whole thing out. "Dad?" I said as I stood up.

Both my parents lowered their newspapers.

"What?" my dad said.

I chickened out. "I'm going over to Stuart's," I said.

My father said, "Just so I understand: You will be at Stuart's tonight?"

"I'll be with Stuart."

"What's that supposed to mean?"

"Never mind," I said, and took off, thinking, *Why do I have to have parents who trust me?*

By the time I got to Stuart's, the guys were all waiting in the lobby. Mr. Lowe met us at the elevator, and we rode up in silence to the thirty-third floor.

"Okay," said Mr. Lowe when they tuned up and we were ready to go. "I don't want to put a lot of pressure on you guys, but let me ask you something. Are you really serious about this gig?"

"Yeah, man," said Tommy.

"We are, dude, we are," agreed Albert.

Stuart just nodded.

I didn't say anything. I was not serious, just panicky. How was I going to get out of this?

"Because," said Mr. Lowe, "this is an incredible opportunity. I'm talking about Jason Bartlebye. The record company man. I'm not sure you fully understand who he is. If this man thinks you've got something . . ." He shook his head. "All I'm saying is, guys, it's worth working for."

I felt like crying. In fact, I think there *were* tears in my eyes. Not that I said anything. I needed a force field to keep things away from me. And another one to keep things in—like tears, or stupid ideas.

But all the other guys said were things like "Sure, man. We know. That's cool."

"What time does this party begin?" asked Mr. Lowe.

They all looked at me.

"We're supposed to be there at seven."

"Okay. We arrive . . . set up . . . tune up. . . ." Mr. Lowe looked at his watch. "That gives us . . . say . . . about six, seven hours to turn into a band that rocks. Let's go."

22.

MEG

● ○

Saturday.

Party day.

Disaster day.

As the sun rose higher and higher, I lay in bed and watched the wall of my room brighten. My sheets—my favorites, the pink T-shirt material ones—were tangled at my ankles. I tried to sink back into my pillow, back to dreamland. My mom used to say sometimes, when she was tucking me in, "Want to meet in dreamland?" And we would choose where we'd find each other—the book area, on some soft pillows, sometimes on the swings.

It had been a while since we met there.

The yellow outfit was hanging from my closet doorknob.

I turned away from it, toward the window, watching the day go by. I had to think of something: a plan to explain why my brother—Ted—did not show up at the party.

Nothing came to me.

After about an hour my breath was so disgusting I dragged my sorry self to the bathroom. On the counter was a fresh jar of face cleanser, with a terry headband draped over it. Under it was a sheet from Mom's prescription pad and a note:

For Meg—
XOXO, Mom

I just used the regular bar. But I did pull my hair back with the headband and do a little inspection.

Same old Meg. My nose, I noticed, may be spreading out, horrifyingly, to take over even more of my face. One eye was slightly more open than the other. Two rosy pimples were threatening to explode across the vast expanse of my five-head. I took off the headband.

I thought, *No wonder Ted won't be asking me out tonight.*

Well, my ugliness and his nonexistence, both.

The phone rang. I didn't even bother to run for it.

"Meg," yelled Mom. "It's Della! Is she coming to the party tonight?"

Coming?

I ran for the phone and brought it into my room and shut the door, minus a crack.

"Hey, there," I said nervously.

"Hey, there," she answered.

I was so relieved. But then I remembered I was really mad at her. "Hey, what do you mean, so what?" I was furious, but I kept my voice quiet and low, like Kimberly's.

"Huh?"

"On your e-mail," I whispered. "What was that supposed to mean?"

"I can't hear you," she said. "You okay, pal? Speak up!"

Though I felt like crying, I laughed. "I miss you," I said.

"I miss you, too. I told you not to go to that fat-brain school. I think it's got you all messed up. You're leaving me these weird messages and incomplete e-mails, and going to sleep before any decent TV shows, and then, well, I should let you explain. What *is* up with you, girl?"

"So much," I started, relieved. I couldn't wait to tell her the whole crazy story.

"So I hear," she said.

"What do you mean?"

"Well, I was planning to invite you for a sleepover tonight, with me, Sarah, Trina, Becky, Lucy, and Sophie—you know, old times—but Lucy said her cousin Hannah's friend Emily is in your smarty-pants school and there's like this *huge* party everybody is going crazy about and some fantastic band called Never Mind is playing at it, and everybody is getting asked out all over the place, and you are supposedly at the center of it all."

I closed my eyes. The wackos who say the end of the world is coming were right after all.

"So?" she said. "Is it true?"

I said, "I have no idea what's true anymore."

"How very world weary of you."

"Della . . ."

"Meg," she said. "You know, you said a lot of stuff this summer about not losing your old friends and everything. Not getting stuck-up and too good for me and your other old friends. Did you even *think* of inviting us to this party of yours?"

"It's not mine!"

"Well, Lucy's cousin Hannah's friend Emily says you are pretty much in charge. And what we want to know . . ."

"We?"

"Yeah, we. Me, Sarah, Trina, Becky, Lucy, and Sophie— remember us? You used to be a part of we. But what we want to know is, are we invited, or not?"

"I was thinking of not going myself."

"Why?"

"I'd rather see you."

"Well, invite us instead."

Why the heck not. What was Kimberly going to do, kick me out of her stupid club for inviting my old friends? Well, she could add it to her list of reasons. "Okay," I said. "You're invited."

"Oh," said Della. "Okay. You're not just saying that because I'm forcing you?"

"Well," I said. "Sort of."

She laughed.

"But I really need to see your face."

"Yeah," said Della. "It's that kind of face. So now give me the dirt—are you really going out with Phelps Bartlebye?"

My turn to laugh. "Your spies have faulty info, Della."

"Well," said Della. "Trina's brother's friend's cousin is friends with him, Phelps, and supposedly he is asking you out, either yesterday or today. And your mom said so too."

"Right."

"Well, sort of. You know how she goes on and on. She

143

was confused about his name, but what the heck kind of name is Phelps, anyway? So I didn't correct her. But, yeah. So if you're not already going out with him, sounds like tonight's the night. Get ready, girl. Where's the party?"

"Um, let me look," I said, searching through my school directory for the right address.

"Hey," said Della, just as I pulled the list out. "You want to hear something funny?"

"You have no idea how much I want to hear something funny," I told her.

"There's also a rumor going around that your brother is going out with Kimberly Wu Woodson, the tennis player."

"Edward?" I asked, feeling so dizzy I had to sit down.

"I know! I love rumors, don't you? Can you imagine? As if a girl like that would ever speak to any of us, never mind Edward!"

I tried to laugh. Couldn't. "You want to hear something *really* funny?" My voice sounded completely unfamiliar to me, all shaky and whispery. "The party? It's at that girl, Kimberly's, apartment."

No sound for I don't know how long, then, "You putting me on?"

"It's true! Kimberly Wu Woodson. Eight P.M. Ten-forty-five Park Avenue. Twelve-E."

Again, a pause. Then: "Park Avenue?"

"Yeah."

"And where's that at, like, in the eighties?"

"I don't know."

"Is she . . . a friend of yours?"

"I guess. She's nice. You'd hate her."

Della was apparently in shock, because she didn't say anything.

"Della?"

She started to giggle, then asked, "So I guess Edward will be there too. Since he's her date?"

"You know, you really are funny."

"Yeah, but funny is only skin-deep. Hey, I'm glad I'll be seeing you tonight, even if it has to be at some stuck-up East Sider's stuffy party, and even if you're going to be Phelps Bartlebye's new conquest. I miss you."

I sniffled. "I miss me too."

I hung up.

I turned down French toast for breakfast and they let me. Mom and Dad both kept looking at me kind of sweetly, wistfully, like, *Oh, my goodness, our little girl is growing up.* They were giving me wide berth and a lot of slack.

"Where's Edward?" I asked.

"At Stuart's," my dad said.

Good, I thought. One good thing about the day. At least I won't have to deal with him. Just with myself. Which at that point was no bargain either.

I took a shower.

Brushed my teeth again.

I used the facial cleanser.

I popped the two zits, one incompletely.

I blew my hair dry.

I used Mom's mascara.

It poked me in the eye, the eye that had been open more than the other earlier, and then, because of diminished vision, using only my one squinty Cyclops eye, clonked the wand under my nose, which made me look like Charlie Chaplin.

I washed it off and started over.

I loaded concealer on top of the swelling half-zit, creating a moonscape effect.

I put on the ugly yellow thing, took it off, put on every other combination of clothes from my closet, then had to excavate and begin again. *What would Kimberly wear?*

23.

EDWARD

● ○

It was a grueling day. Because we worked. I mean, really worked. With nothing but a lunch break, which was short.

But it was during the break that Stuart came up to me. "Gotta hand it to you."

"What for?"

"Sticking with this," he said. "I thought you were going to bag it."

"No way," I mumbled.

"Cool," he said.

Which pretty much ruined my idea of sneaking off while the rest of them ate.

At about five o clock Mr. Lowe—who had stayed with us all day—said, "I think we should quit. We've got five songs. That'll have to do." He sat there in his chair, looking down, bald head resting in his hands.

It was Stuart who said, "Mr. Lowe . . . we any good?"

Mr. Lowe looked up. Sort of nodded. "I'll never lie to you kids. That's what I promised you. Won't start now. Are you any good? Not as good as you will be.

But you've worked hard. Real hard. I give you a lot of credit. I'm proud of you. I say we go and do the best we can. Hey, I do believe in miracles. I truly do."

He looked at us and stood up. "Let's do it," he said.

If he had said, "Let's open these windows and jump toward the Hudson River," I would have gone right along. Happily. But instead we were on our way to Kimberly's party—which was far worse.

24.

MEG

● ○

When Mom said, "Meg, time to go!" I happened to be in my low-rise pinkish overdyed jeans, which are slightly too tight, and the ugly yellow top, again. I was just giving it one last chance.

"I can't go like this!"

"You look terrific," Mom said, yanking the tags off the shirt. "Which is more than I can say for this room."

"I have to change! I look like Big Bird."

She laughed, then dragged me out, literally by my hair. "Come on, come on. It's not how you look but who you are that really matters."

Who I am? And that would be . . . ???

I still had no plan.

SATURDAY
NIGHT:
THE PARTY

25.

EDWARD

● ○

Mr. Lowe backed his van up behind the apartment house. We loaded all the equipment, which wasn't easy because we had to lug all the stuff—including the drums—to the freight elevator, through some long, dark corridors and across the courtyard of Stuart's building to where he'd parked.

But we did it.

It was only when we got that done that Tommy suddenly said, "Hey, we going to be dressed the way we are?"

We all looked to Mr. Lowe. He seemed embarrassed. "You know," he said, "I forgot all about that."

I did a quick survey. Mr. Lowe was in overalls. There was Stuart, in chinos and a T-shirt that read "May the Moss Be with You," plus his lopsided eyeglasses. Tommy was dressed in his big baggie stuff, all black. Albert had jeans, big army boots, and a sweatshirt with the words "Manhattan Maybes" and the numbers zero—zero on it. I had on my cargos and a T-shirt with a picture of Excalibur, King Arthur's magic sword.

Mr. Lowe broke into a grin. "Hey," he said, "it's the music that counts."

After Stuart went back upstairs for a quick good-bye to his folks, we all piled in, with Mr. Lowe behind the wheel.

We were sitting there, sort of tense, when Mr. Lowe cried out, "How we doing?"

Like a chorus, they all yelled, "Never Mind!" That cracked them up. I say "them," because I couldn't say anything. My mouth was too dry.

All I could think was, *How do I get out of this?* It was going to be a disaster. Meg was going to kill me. My parents were going to kill me. And I would be next in line to kill me too.

Mr. Lowe put the van in gear and off we went.

He headed east on Sixty-third Street and then, at the light, asked, "Hey, where we going?"

I had some thoughts on the subject, but they weren't what some adults might call appropriate. "Oh," I mumbled. "I forgot the paper with the address thing." Lame way out, but I was willing to go for any escape by then.

Tommy pulled the crumpled paper out of his pocket. "I got it, bone-head." He read the address to Mr. Lowe and then crumpled it back up and threw it at my head.

We went left on Central Park West. I stared out the window at the glittering lights of Tavern on the Green as we took a right and headed into Central Park. I normally love riding through the park. Not this time.

It didn't take long for us to pull up to Kimberly's apartment. It was a big building and looked fancy. A doorman with white gloves and gold spaghetti on his shoulders opened the passenger side door.

We climbed out.

"We've been expecting you," the doorman said, all cool, like this was some perfectly normal arrival. "We have a cart ready." He went to get it.

"What time we supposed to be here?" said Stuart.

"Seven," I reminded him. I thought of just walking off. Started to. Stuart grabbed me and laughed. Thought it was a joke. Ha!

Tommy checked his watch. "It's only six-thirty," he said.

"Trust me," said Mr. Lowe. "When it comes to setting up, there's no such thing as being too early. How big is her apartment?"

They all looked to me.

"Never saw it."

There was a moment of silence. The kind of silence that meant, as my father liked to say, the angel of death was flying low.

"And this girl . . . who's giving the party. Your friend. What's her name?"

"My sister's friend," I said.

"Dimberly," said Stuart.

I said, "Actually, Kimberly."

The doorman reappeared with his cart. "Miss Woodson's apartment is on the twelfth floor. She is very excited."

I'm thinking, *Why are all these adults helping me? Shouldn't they be hating teenagers?*

Albert, with a grin, says, "Check. Kimberly Woodson."

"Let's unload," said Mr. Lowe.

We did, with the doorman's help. He put all our stuff on his cart with carpeting on the bottom and a gold arch over the top.

Mr. Lowe handed the doorman some bills. Good thing he was with us. I wouldn't have known you had to pay the guy.

The doorman waited for the elevator with us. When it came, it was, unfortunately, a big one. We were able to get everything and everyone—including me—onto it.

We zipped up to the twelfth floor. Too fast.

I was nervous but, by then, I could tell, so was everyone.

We unloaded from the elevator and lugged everything to the door that was marked twelve-E.

"This it?" asked Stuart, looking at me through his cockeyed glasses.

I said, "Maybe I should go back to the car, check that address."

"This is it," the doorman said. *Thanks, pal.*

Albert shoved me toward the door. "Ring it," he growled.

They waited for me to push the bell. Which, after maybe ten years, I did. From deep inside the apartment, we heard a ding-dong. The door opened.

I looked up at this girl standing there. If I thought Meg was tall, this girl was Mount Everest. She had smooth black hair, with a tan, oval face. And I have to say—pretty. Seriously good looking, like from a magazine. With a lot of makeup, mostly around her eyes. She was wearing this kind of coat. Or maybe it was a robe.

She stared at us. "Oh my God," she said.

And I said, "Hi."

She looked down at me. Way down. "And you are . . . ?" she said.

I said, "Never Mind."

"Oh my God," she said again, sort of clutching the neck of her coat. You could see her eyes go over all of us, one at a time. Searching for I knew who.

"The . . . *band*?" she said.

"Yup," said Albert.

She moved back a couple of steps. "And . . . Ted?" she whispered. "Which is . . . Ted?"

Since no one knew that was me—except me—and I didn't want to know either—there was a lot of silence until I heard myself say, "Ted? Oh, he'll be here later. When we . . . set up."

"Oh," she said. "He didn't mention he was sending . . . I told him seven."

I shrugged.

"Kimberly!" came a voice from somewhere inside the apartment. "Who is that?"

"Some people from the band. Roadies. To set up!" she called back.

"Do they really have to come so early?" came the voice.

Mr. Lowe stepped forward. "Apologize for the inconvenience, but it does take a while to arrange things. . . ."

"They have to come in!" Kimberly screamed to the mystery voice.

"Oh, all right."

Kimberly stepped aside.

Mr. Lowe held out his hand. "I'm Carl Lowe. And you are . . . Kimberly?"

"Yeah," she said, not shaking his hand but hugging herself. "Who are you?

"The boys' manager."

"Oh."

We came into a kind of front room. There was a table with a big flower arrangement on it, surrounded by musical note confetti, and a mirror on the wall above. I saw us reflected in it. We looked pretty creepy.

"Go in there," Kimberly said, pointing. "The big room. When will Ted be here?" she asked.

"Pretty soon," I said, wishing she would get off the Ted subject.

"You can go ahead and set up," she said, and flashed us a smile. Man, she was like, seriously hot. "We're still dressing."

With that, she turned and went down a hall.

We stood there.

"That Kimberly?" asked Albert.

I said, "I guess."

"She's got attitude," Tommy announced.

"As well as altitude," said Stuart.

"Who is this . . . Ted?" Mr. Lowe asked.

"How should I know?" I said.

"Well," he said, smiling. "Let's go."

We went in the direction Kimberly had pointed out and came into this big room. It was pretty empty, but hanging on the far wall was a huge poster, which read:

NEVER MIND!!!

That stopped us all for a few seconds. It looked professionally made. I made myself gaze around, to get my eyes off the poster. Fancy wood floor. Dark wood-paneled walls. Fireplace, swept clean. Huge windows hung with major curtains. Against one wall was a long table on which was a tablecloth and food. Heaps of it. Soda. Cookies. Chips. Olympic-sized pools of dip.

"Whoa," cried Stuart, moving toward the table. "Look at all this food."

"Whoa yourself!" said Mr. Lowe. "Respect that young lady's wishes. Let's set up."

Tommy, Albert, and Mr. Lowe started laying out their stuff.

Since I was the lead singer, there wasn't much for me to do. Then I realized this was my moment: I could just walk out. Be gone. Free. "I'm going to find a bathroom," I said, sort of whispering because my heart was really pounding.

When no one said anything, I turned and started for the front door. But as I approached it I saw, reflected in the mirror, a girl.

She looked about nine. She was dressed in a dirty T-shirt and jeans. Bare feet.

"Hi," she said.

"Hi," I returned to her reflection, then stepped into the hallway to see her in person. She was leaning against the front door. Like a guard. Blocking my escape.

"Who are you?" she asked.

"Ah . . . Edward. And you?"

"Brett. Kimberly's sister. Hard to believe, right? Everyone says that. You probably think I'm like nine or something."

I shook my head. "I was thinking more like . . . eleven."

She smiled. "Ten and a half. Are you in the band?"

"Yeah."

"You're not Ted, are you?"

"Ahh . . . he's not here yet."

"Do you know him?"

"Ah . . . I guess."

"Do you know his twin sister?"

"Yeah." I was just standing there, wishing the girl would go away. She had multicolored braces on her teeth, like me. She was small and scrawny. I could've pushed her, but I don't normally push little girls, and besides, that would've attracted more attention than I needed. Instead I leaned against the wall.

"Can I ask you something?" she said.

"What?" She was staring at my hand. I took it off the wall. I'd left a smudge. I tried to rub it off. That made it worse. I stood in front of it.

"My sister thinks Ted Runyon's sister is a simple nothing who would make an obedient secretary but that Ted is the most perfect human being in the whole world."

"How do you know?"

"I listen to her phone calls—secretly. What do you think of Ted's sister?"

I said, "I like her."

She grinned. "I bet I will too, then." Then she said, "Ted may be famous, but he must be *so* stupid."

"Why?"

She came up to me and whispered into my ear, "He likes my sister."

"I don't," I blurted out.

She looked up at me, hands on her hips. "You know what?"

"What?"

"I like you. And your braces." Then she added, "But if you are part of the band, how come you were trying to sneak out?"

I looked at Kimberly's kid sister. "What makes you think I'm sneaking out?"

"You are, aren't you?"

I stood there completely at a loss. Caught.

Then this girl, Brett, said, "I wish you wouldn't go."

"Why?"

"Because I bet you're better than any Ted."

She had a point. But there was nothing I could do. I was trapped in the apartment, no way out. So I said, "Yeah, well. You're right."

She said, "Want to see something funny?"

"I'd love it," I answered.

"If I go out and ring the doorbell, my sister will go nuts when she sees it's just me."

"I bet," I said, turned around, and headed back to the band.

26.

MEG

● ○

As Mom was dragging me out the door and Dad was already standing by the elevator, the phone rang. Mom said, "It could be Grandma." She ran back to the kitchen.

"Is Grandma coming too?" I shrieked.

Dad laughed but didn't actually say no.

"Is she?" I really did scream.

"Meg!" Dad shook his head. "No. She's not. I think she's playing in a tennis tournament tonight. Believe it or not, there is a world beyond this party." He massaged my shoulders, which were up past my earlobes again, and whispered, "Relax, huh, champ?"

From the kitchen Mom yelled, "Meg?"

I eyed Dad furiously and went in to take the phone from her.

Mom had her hand over the mouthpiece. "Whoever it is, she sure speaks quietly," Mom whispered. "And she thought Ted might be here. Is Ted coming by to go to the party with us?"

It had to be Kimberly. "What did you tell her?" I asked, panicked.

"I just said, 'Ted's not here right now, would you like to

speak with Meg?'" she answered. "Is that okay? Was I cool? Did I do it right?"

I managed to nod. Mom kissed my cheek and handed me the phone.

"Hello?" My own voice was not much more than a whisper.

"Meg?" Kimberly, whispering too. "Did Ted leave already?"

"Um, yeah," I said, thinking, *Hey, maybe Ted and the guys could get into a car accident or, no, that would be on the news—maybe one of the guys would be sick and, or, no . . . Yikes.* "Yeah," I repeated weakly. The yellow fabric under my arms was damp. Oh, yes, I am a glamour queen.

"So he should be here soon?" Kimberly asked.

I don't know if it was the anxiety in her voice that calmed me down and got me to think of a way out, or if my plan was so obvious it would've come to me eventually no matter what. "Should be," I said, feeling a smile begin to raise my mouth corners. "In fact, they should be there already."

I smiled at the elegance of the plan. I would just act as surprised as everybody else that Ted and his band never showed up, and that would give me until Monday to come up with a new lie.

Okay, so it wasn't a solution. It was lame and only put off my ultimate exposure and humiliation. But at that point I was truly psyched to think I might be able to engineer a thirty-six-hour delay. So I added, trying to sound concerned, "I wonder where those guys could be?"

"No," whispered Kimberly. "I mean just him. The rest of the band is here already."

There was a moment of silence during which the universe shook, I am pretty sure.

"The band is *there*?" I think I said. My sweat glands, having enjoyed a fifteen-second break, pumped back in action. *What band could she mean?*

"Yeah," whispered Kimberly. "They've been setting up and tuning their instruments for a whole *hour*."

"But . . . who is there?" Sweat was actually running down from my armpits to the tight waist of my jeans and pooling there. I was melting, while imitating an owl. "Who . . . who?"

"Never Mind," she whispered, and giggled. "I mean, you know, the band Never Mind. A roadie said Ted told them he'd be along later. But I can't remember what you said their names are. You know, the guys in the band."

I was at a total loss. Who in the world could be in Kimberly's apartment, setting up instruments and telling her "Ted" would be along soon? Imaginary people don't normally pop out of my head and into people's living rooms. Unless, I started thinking—a lot of people have heard about this party. Those guys in Kimberly's apartment could be anybody. They could be criminals who'd heard about the party like everybody else in Manhattan. What were they going to do, blow up the place? Or worse? I had to say something. "But . . . Kimberly?" My throat was suddenly so dry my voice had trouble getting out. I was scorched on the inside and liquefying on the outside. I coughed a bit and then managed to ask, "What do these guys, the, um, band, look like?"

"Not exactly as you'd implied they'd look, as I'm sure you know."

I had no answer. I touched my head to see if I was running a fever only to realize that my hair, which was drenched, was beginning to frizz. (My hair, of course, was the least of my problems right then, but still . . .)

Kimberly giggled. It didn't sound as cool as it used to. I didn't join in.

"Anyway," she whispered. "It doesn't matter to me what they look like because Ted is the . . . Oh, that's the doorbell. That must be Ted. See you soon!"

She hung up on me.

I stood there, holding on to the phone, wondering, *What is going on?*

"Everything okay?" my dad asked, coming down the hall.

"I don't know."

"Is Ted coming here?" Mom asked.

"We'd be happy to give him a lift," Dad added.

"No," I snapped, then, feeling almost as sorry for them as I was for myself, added, "Ted . . . seems to be going on his own."

27.

EDWARD

● ○

"Can we eat now?" Stuart asked Mr. Lowe when everything was set up.

"Come on, Stuart, we still need to do some sound checks."

The doorbell rang. Everybody froze. Kimberly ran by. Then we heard her scream, "Brett!"

Next minute Brett came into the room, looked at me, and winked. I managed to grin.

The whole time we did the checks, one instrument at a time, Brett hung out, watching, right next to me, as if she was my best friend. Or my guardian. Or my guard.

We were almost done when Kimberly returned. She wasn't really so dressed up, just wearing jeans and a shirt, but she didn't look like anybody I've ever seen wearing jeans and a shirt before. All of us just stared at her. You could see a hint of her belly button. My neck felt hot.

Hands on her hips, she demanded, "Why isn't Ted here yet?"

"Ted?" said Albert. "Who *is* this dude?"

"*Very, very* funny," Kimberly said. Then she gave a

forced smile. "He happens to be my boyfriend! Brett, will you get out of here!" She turned on her heels and stormed out of the room.

"Lucky Ted," murmured Tommy under his breath, which made everyone but me laugh. I mean, I didn't think I was lucky.

Brett announced, "I think Ted is a jerk."

We all laughed, some (me) harder than others.

The next one to appear was an older woman. She said, "Hello. I'm Emily Wu, Kimberly's mother. We're very happy you're here. Very excited." Actually, she looked worried.

"Thank you," said Mr. Lowe, shaking her hand. "I'm Carl Lowe. The boys' manager. Nice of you to have us here. They're excited too."

"Thank you, Mr. Lowe. I'm sorry that Mr. Woodson is missing this. But he's away on a business trip. Well, there's food. Please help yourselves. Anything I can get for you?" Ms. Wu asked.

Stuart shot over to the table and started grabbing.

Mr. Lowe smiled. "An audience."

As he said that, the doorbell rang. "There you are!" chimed Ms. Wu. She headed for the door. We listened.

Ms. Wu: "Yes?"

A voice: "This the Never Mind party?"

Ms. Wu: "Well . . ."

The next second some twenty or so kids swarmed in. And the thing of it was, they were from *our* school—the Charlton Street Alternative School. What's more, they were wearing the wildest, far-out getups you could imagine. Talk about alternative. There was more different-colored hair than in a box of Crayola crayons. There were earrings, nose rings, belly-button rings, tattoos (fake, because I know those kids didn't have them at school the day before).

From the look on Ms. Wu's face, I could see she was a bit startled. But she was trying hard to be nice. "There's food, everybody," she announced. "Please help yourselves."

The kids rushed toward us, laughing and shouting. Tommy and Albert (and even Stuart) greeted them like old friends, which they probably were. They even said hello to me, as if they knew me.

Brett tugged on my sleeve and said, "I like that girl with the pink and purple hair. Do you?"

"I guess."

"Don't worry. I still like you better."

I felt my face get red. "Thanks."

And in the back, I could see Kimberly. She was acting as if she was not sure what was happening.

So for that one moment, she and I had something in common.

28.

MEG

●○

The sidewalk in front of Kimberly's apartment was clogged with town cars and cabs, kids spilling out of them, laughing, chatting, waving good-bye to parents who opened windows and called out last-minute reminders about pickup times and "I love you's."

Dad told our cab driver he could let us out at the corner.

"I can go up myself," I told them.

"Your mother has to use the bathroom," Dad said.

"She does not," I said.

Mom was getting out of the cab on the other side. "What?" she asked, then looked at my dad and said, "Oh, right, I have to use the bathroom. We'll just run up with you. I'm sure they won't mind, right? What are these people's names?"

"Woodson," I mumbled. "Wu."

"What?"

"I don't know."

Feeling like a hostage, I headed toward the building.

We rode up in the elevator with a whole gang of kids. My parents were the only ones over fifteen. One of the pretty girls said, over the din of other kids, "Hey, Meg?"

"What?" I asked.

Mom smiled encouragingly at the girl.

The girl leaned toward me. "Is it true you're going out with Phelps?"

29.

EDWARD

● ○

I thought the room was crowded when all the kids from my school came in. But over the next ten minutes so many more came that it really got packed. Not that I recognized them. I guessed they were from Meg's school. The place was more like a school lunchroom— at lunchtime. The kids swarmed over the food table like an alien fungus in a science fiction movie. I mean, they devoured it.

The only open space was where Never Mind was set up. And even there kids kept edging in. There was all this noise, too, and it was getting louder and more crowded second by second. I was really feeling sick. There was no getting out of it now.

Somehow Kimberly managed to squeeze through everybody. "Isn't Ted here yet?" she asked. "Brett, would you go to your room! This is *my* party!"

By this time the other guys were getting into this notion of "Ted." So it was Tommy who said, "Hey, girl, let me warn you about Ted. He's as dependable as a yo-yo on a slack string."

I saw tears well up in Kimberly's eyes. "But he *is* coming, isn't he?"

Stuart, grinning, said, "Wasn't he going to Hollywood this afternoon?" He banged his bass drum to make the point.

"Hollywood?" cried Kimberly.

"You mean London," said Albert, plucking a string.

"I thought it was Nashville," added Tommy. *Bong.*

"Ha ha!" said Brett, who was sitting cross-legged by my feet. "I hope he never comes."

Kimberly's mother broke through the raucous crowd. She was looking frazzled.

"Boys," she said, "I think you had better start playing. I don't want to have things get out of hand. Is that possible?" The last she said to Mr. Lowe.

Mr. Lowe looked around and nodded. "I think that might be a good idea." To us, in an undertone, he said, "Jason Bartlebye just arrived."

"But what about Ted?" wailed Kimberly.

"He went to the moon!" Brett shouted.

30.

MEG

● ○

"Phelps?" asked Dad. "Who's Phelps? I thought you like a boy named . . ."

"Dad!" I screamed. He could *not*, under any circumstances, be allowed to announce that I liked Ted, who they all thought was my twin brother! "Mom," I begged. "Please . . ."

Mom put her hand on Dad's arm as the elevator door slid open. There was a small foyer, marble and mirrors, and two doors—12-E and 12-W. East and West. These were going to be some big-time, fancy apartments. I had heard about these but, in all my twelve years of living in Manhattan, had never been inside one.

I turned to check Mom's reaction. At that moment the door to the apartment flew open. Kimberly stood there, looking even more gorgeous than usual in her low-rise black pants and a white button-down men's shirt, tied at the waist. I should've worn the black pants, I realized. And a white shirt. Why am I in yellow? Why is my shirt tucked into too-tight jeans? Why, even when my life is about to end, do I have to look like a dork?

Kimberly looked over the crowd of us, spotted me, and

reached over the heads of two seventh-grade girls to grab my arm. "Meg!"

She pulled me into the apartment, past everybody, away from my parents, into a big room with a NEVER MIND!!! banner strung up over the heads of a huge swarm of kids I didn't recognize, and one that I did.

Edward.

31.

EDWARD

● ○

Kimberly's mother turned to face the crowd. "Okay, everybody," she all but shouted. "The band is going to play."

There were squeals, shouts, and a few calls like "Go for it!" Even Brett moved off a bit.

"Let's go, guys," said Mr. Lowe to us.

We got into position, instruments on the ready. As for me, there I was, right up front, legs shaking, gulping for air, knowing that without any doubt I was going to have to sing.

Which is when I saw Meg and my parents come into the room.

32.

MEG

● ○

Edward was standing in front of a microphone.

"Hon, take a peek over there," I heard Mom say. She was pointing at Edward and looking as shocked as I felt nauseated.

Dad squinted through his glasses and mumbled, "What the . . ."

I looked back to where Edward was standing. There were two strange-looking guys flanking him, both with those eighth-grade-see-I've-begun-puberty goatees smudging their chins. One had green hair hanging over his face like a lost leaf. Behind the three of them, with his goofball glasses riding his nose and crusty gunk smeared on his pudgy cheeks, was Edward's gross and only friend, Stuart Barcaster. He was twitching behind a drum set like some fairy tale troll under a bridge.

I don't know if the room had gotten quiet or if my brain had just clicked off the sound. I made eye contact with Edward.

He looked petrified.

Blinking and frowning, he was clutching the microphone stand. Being so scrawny, he could practically hide behind it.

Part of me wanted to scream at him, "Get out of my party! Get out of my life, you freak, you barnacle, you onion! You ruin everything!"

But another part of me, most of me, really, sort of had to think, *Well, there he is*. This is crazy: there—just as I had said—is my twin brother, at the head of the band Never Mind. Out of my imagination into an East Side living room. Maybe it was a fairy tale. Except suddenly Kimberly, beside me, screamed in my ear, "Meg, I want the truth!"

I mumbled, "I doubt it."

"Did Ted really go to Hollywood?"

"Um," I said, thinking, *Huh? Who said anything about Hollywood?* "Do you *think* he went to Hollywood?"

"That's the rumor." Kimberly groaned. "Some huge movie deal. But I don't believe it."

I smiled at her. I almost actually said, "Congratulations, Sherlock," but then I heard Stuart's drumsticks click together and his liitle boy's voice squeak, "One, two, one two three . . ."

And in those five seconds, I looked back at Edward.

He shrugged.

I felt myself smile at him.

He actually smiled back, a little, and opened his mouth, and that's when I realized, *Oh my God*—my twin brother is actually going to *sing*.

33.

EDWARD

● ○

The only thing I could think about were the people in front of me. Like, the whole frigging twelve-year-old population of New York City! All these kids, from my school, as well as lots I didn't know from I didn't know where, crowded close together. They were squealing, shouting, shoving and pushing, pulsing to the beat. Not too far away, on the floor, was Brett, gazing at me, clapping her hands. Kimberly stood alone with these black smudges running down her cheeks so that she looked like one of those pathetic clowns that you laugh at. Kimberly's mother was pinch faced, fake smiling, obviously unsure if all was good or all a disaster. Mr. Lowe was standing next to this tall guy, the only one in the whole room with a suit and necktie. I figured him to be Mr. Jason Bartlebye.

And my parents were there too, staring at me, their mouths actually hanging open. And coming in the door was Meg's best friend, Della, from our old school, and *her* whole crowd. A few of those girls started waving at me. Waving and cheering and pointing me out to each other, not meanly but like, happy to see me, and one of them, Trina, who actually was *my* friend back in second grade—I am pretty sure she was yelling, "Rock on, Edward!"

But the most amazing thing (for me) was Meg. Because she was looking right at me and what she did was . . . she smiled.

I might have smiled back—I'm not sure.

I say I'm not sure because behind me the music was starting to build like a vomiting volcano. When I looked behind me, there was Stuart, sweat already pouring down his face, with his lopsided eyeglasses and a grin on his face to match, so that he looked positively wicked as he slammed away on his drums.

As for Albert and Tommy, they were jumping up and down, doing something like—I don't know what—a kind of dance, I suppose. Albert's green streak of hair was bopping around like a sick metronome gone wild. Tommy had his eyes sort of closed, and he was leaning back, or doing whatever it was he was doing—I wasn't sure what it was.

Then it came to me—they were having fun. What's more, I realized all these people out front were looking at me and most of them—except maybe Kimberly and her mother—were also having fun. The thing is I actually remember telling myself, *You are not a rock star. Everybody knows that. We stink. Think of it as a movie so bad it's funny.* Pretend *you are a rock star. No one really cares— except maybe Kimberly. So hey, may as well go for it!*

I had this surge of energy—maybe it was just desperation—but I grabbed the microphone the way I've seen them do it on TV. What's more, I began to sing, or maybe, to be honest, I was just shouting out the words.

I don't even remember what I sang.

All I know is that when I started to sing, everything went bug-out crazy. Of course I also noticed that Mr. Lowe had his hands in front of his face—hiding. So I knew we must have been pretty awful. That record guy, Bartlebye, he was actually *laughing*.

But the kids were going nuts. A complete freak-out. Maybe a hundred kids packed tight jumping, swaying, hands up, having *fun*. And the most amazing thing of all was that I was having fun too.

And then there was Meg. For a moment she was frozen. But then I actually saw her start clapping, rocking out, laughing, but like, how she used to laugh. Not fake. Like she really was happy. Like she was having a grand old time. Like she was *loving* it.

So we just went on from song to song—each one louder and wilder—until I saw, at the back of the crowd, a policeman.

34.

MEG

●　○

They were bad.

I mean really bad, not like slang *bad* which means "good." I mean bad as in real bad. As in just really loud noise.

But they were also great. As in fun.

They were so far out there, so wacky, so totally goofy and having such a great time, we all went nuts. It was easy to sing along because for one thing it was so incredibly *loud* you felt like the music—if you want to call it that— was already in your head, already in your heart and moving your mouth so you just felt like letting it out. Besides, how could anybody be self-conscious when Edward and his wacko band were making being totally insane look like so much . . . life?

Mom started to laugh. Dad whooped. All around me people were screaming, clapping, singing. Annabelle clomped through the crowd and screamed in my ear, "They are so awesome!"

I have no idea if she was being ironic or if she was severely tone deaf or if she had an appreciation for what was going on that went way beyond music and way, way beyond what I had thought of her and her bland niceness until that moment. But I just shrieked back, "I know it!"

I started clapping. I did it above my head, so Edward, if he decided to open his eyes, would see.

I didn't notice the whistle was not coming from up front, at least for a while.

Somebody had called the police, a neighbor, I guess. You could understand why: It was like an earthquake in a seashell in there.

The band stopped playing or somebody pulled the plug on their equipment. This cop announced that the party was over and that, please, folks, you need to make your way out in an orderly fashion and don't overload the elevator, thank you.

It was crazy. People crying that their parents were at the movies and wouldn't be back to pick them up until eleven, some kids grumbling about their First Amendment rights, and a lot of kids chanting, "Never Mind, Never Mind." I think Mom joined in, quietly, on that. Not sure what *she* meant.

Through the crush, I felt someone grab my wrist. I looked up and there was Della. Just as I was reaching to hug her, though, Kimberly grabbed my other hand.

35.

EDWARD

● ○

The music was over. The room started getting empty pretty fast, considering how many people had been in there. Stuart was at the food table, scrounging for last bits. He wasn't alone. His mom and stepfather were with him, telling him how great he was, and he was grinning—or was he just trying to keep the food in? Albert and Tommy were talking excitedly to each other, giving each other so many high fives it looked like they were playing patty cake.

I felt a tug on my sleeve. It was Brett.

"That was so cool," she said. Next second she flung her arms around me, gave me a hug, turned bright red, and ran off.

Mr. Lowe, with Mr. Bartlebye, came up. "Guys!" he called. "Stuart! Let go of the food a sec!"

We all gathered around. "Hey," said Mr. Lowe, "that was fun. Let me introduce you to Jason Bartlebye."

The guy grinned. "Boys, that was one of the best takeoffs on a band I've seen and heard in a long time. Really made me laugh. Great job!" With that he turned and moved away. We never saw him again.

For a moment we just stood there. It was Tommy who said to Mr. Lowe, "That bad?"

Mr. Lowe nodded. "No miracles this time. But, hey, you had fun. Everyone had fun. It was a good experience. So we go on from here. What do you say?"

As if we had been trained to do it, we all (including me) shouted, "Never Mind!"

Mr. Lowe grinned, shook his head, and wandered away. I saw him talking to Kimberly's mother. I think he was consoling her.

My parents were coming toward me. But I wasn't really looking at them. I was watching Meg, who was standing between Della and Kimberly. Above the din I could hear Kimberly shrieking, "Will someone *please* tell me where Ted is?"

36.

MEG

● ○

Della and Kimberly stared at each other, each one holding one of my wrists. At the same instant, they both asked, "Who is *she*?"

"My friend," I said meekly to both. Neither let go of my wrists.

"Whatever," said Kimberly. "Where's your twin brother?"

"He's right over there," said Della, pointing toward the band area. Kimberly and I both looked. Luckily the crowd was swarming and, even more lucky, Edward is so short he was hidden. But I knew that might not last. The crowd, that is. I have never been so tense as I was right then.

"He's here?" shrieked Kimberly.

"Yeah," Della answered. "He was right over—somewhere over—you actually know him?"

"Know him?" Kimberly cocked her head and peered down snidely at Della. "I happen to be going out with him."

Della blinked slowly. Then she looked Kimberly over. I figured she was probably thinking, *But you are gorgeous! And huge! And you're going out with little Onion?* But all she said was, "No way."

Kimberly blushed, purple. She swallowed twice and

tugged at her little white shirt, then spat out, "Who *are* you? You come to my home and start insulting me? Maybe I'm not as brilliant a musician as Ted, or the most beautiful girl in the world, but . . ."

"Ted?" Della asked.

"That's what his *friends* call him," Kimberly retorted. "You probably call him Edward."

"I used to." Della shrugged, then mumbled, "Among other things. But people are jerks sometimes." She looked up at me apologetically.

"Who are you calling a jerk?" Kimberly stamped her foot. "Meg, who is this rude girl?"

"My friend," I said, then, louder, "My best friend." And then, spotting Sarah, Trina, Becky, Lucy, and Sophie behind her, I added, "These are all my friends."

Kimberly looked them all over. "These people?"

I nodded.

"Really? They all look like Esther Grossbart."

"Esther is a friend of mine, too."

Kimberly rolled her eyes. "Figures. And you think Phelps Bartlebye likes you? Please. Let's not fool ourselves."

There was nothing I could say to that. I shrugged a little. She was right. I felt about as low as she obviously wanted me to feel.

But then she snorted and went on, "You're probably friends with those losers in the band, too."

"Hey," I said. I felt my eyes narrow and my hands tighten. I leaned toward Kimberly. My whole body clenched, but this

187

time, for once, not from nervousness. For the first time in my life I didn't feel nervous in the slightest. I was just mad. What I was thinking was, *You call my brother a loser, you just bought yourself a kiss from my fist.*

"Hey what?" Kimberly actually looked frightened.

I leaned even closer to Kimberly's face and whispered slowly, "Don't you *dare* use that word about them."

"Lighten up, Meg," Kimberly said, pulling back. "The point is, where's Ted?"

"He was here," said Della, blunt as ever, standing right behind me. "And if he didn't even say hello to you, shouldn't you be asking yourself why?"

Kimberly shrugged nervously and mumbled, "Maybe he didn't see me."

"Yeah?" I said. She was about to get it for every kid I should've given a beating for picking on Edward for the past twelve years. Including myself. "Maybe, Kimberly. Except, you're a little tough to miss. Right? You know what? I've known my twin brother since before we were born. He is probably the bravest, coolest person ever. He *is* here. He is avoiding you. Does that sound like he likes you? Please, let's not fool ourselves."

Kimberly opened her mouth to answer, closed it, and opened it a few more times, looking very much like a goldfish Edward and I once owned. "You can forget the High Achievers Club," she mumbled.

"Oh, darn," I said, and smiled.

Kimberly pushed her way through the crowd and out,

down the hall. Above the din I could hear her door slam. No rules in this family, obviously.

I felt a tug on my sleeve. I looked around. There was this nine-year-old-looking girl in a T-shirt and jeans.

"That was so cool," she said.

"Yeah," I said. "It was. Who are you?"

"Edward's girlfriend," she said, and then disappeared into the crowd.

37.

EDWARD

● ○

Meg, surrounded by her friends from our old school, was, fortunately, keeping Kimberly away from me and the band. But my parents came right on up to me.

It was Dad who said, "Ed, that was hilarious. Really great."

"So funny," my mom joined in. "People loved it. I had no idea you could do that."

I felt like saying, "Me neither," but all I did was just stand there and grin.

Mom squeezed me. "And guess who loved it the most?"

"Who?"

"Your twin sister. Followed closely by us, of course, and then by all Meg's old friends."

My father took me by the shoulder and drew me in a little closer. My mom was right there. "Have you seen that boy," he asked, low voiced. "Meg's boyfriend. Ted?"

"Ted? Her boyfriend is . . . Ted?" I was trying to fit this together. *What about Phelps?*

"Well," whispered Mom. "He's not her boyfriend,

exactly. Just a boy she likes."

"Ted," I repeated.

"Right. She was hoping Ted would, you know, ask her out tonight."

I had to smile. "Really? Ted?"

"I got the feeling from Meg that you knew him," Mom said, head cocked.

"Maybe," I said. "A little."

"*Is* he here?" Mom asked.

I shrugged, noncommittal. Mom and Dad looked worriedly at each other.

"Poor Meg," whispered Mom. "I think she's really disappointed. What should we do?"

I looked past them, toward Meg. She caught my look. She smiled at me.

I turned back to my parents and said, "Actually, I think she's pretty happy he's gone."

38.

MEG

● ○

"It's been kind of a crazy week," I was telling my old friends, with Della still clutching my wrist, when I felt a tap on my shoulder.

I turned around.

Phelps Bartlebye stood there, looking smack into my eyes.

"That was fun," he said.

"Yeah," I managed.

"See ya."

So I said, "See ya," back to him.

He left. Nobody said anything for a second, then everybody, Della, Sarah, Trina, Becky, Lucy, and Sophie, all screamed.

I screamed too. What the heck.

I felt someone touch my hair and spun around.

Mom. "Hi, girls," she said to my friends, and then, softly, "Hey, sweetheart, what happened with Ted?"

"Ted?" asked Della. "Ted is—"

"History," I interrupted, fast.

Edward was passing us, hauling the microphone stand. He stopped.

"Oh?" asked Dad to me.

"Yeah," said Della, smirking at Edward. "That relationship was doomed from the start. That loser is not good enough to be with a Runyon." She cocked her head toward where Kimberly had stormed off.

Edward nodded a quick thanks.

"Absolutely," I said.

Mom pulled my chin toward her to get a look into my eyes, or my soul, to see if I was, god forbid, *hurt*.

"Good riddance to Ted," I said, so happy. Edward laughed, and so did I. "Let's help Edward and his friends out with their stuff."

So we did. My friends are pretty strong. So, it turned out, were Edward's. We made it out in one trip, all together.

39.

EDWARD

● ○

Next morning, I went looking for Meg. She wasn't in her room. Or the kitchen. Found her in the study. She was just sitting there, twirling a strand of hair, sort of folded over one of the big chairs.

I plopped down in the other.

She looked at me. Smiled.

I looked back at her. Grinned.

"So," she said. "What do you think of Ted?"

I said, "I've been thinking about him a lot."

"Yeah?" she asked. "Me, too. And?"

I had to think a sec. "Are we talking about Ted—the boyfriend? Or Ted—the twin brother?"

"You choose."

"Well, Ted the boyfriend. Ah . . . he isn't your type."

She tilted her head. "Which is?"

"Smart," I said. "But maybe a low achiever. And very cool."

"Sounds right," she said. "How about Ted and Kimberly?"

I laughed. "I guess he dumped her."

Meg laughed too. "He was too good for her."

"Too tall anyway," I said. "As for Ted the twin brother . . ."

"No," she said. "I have the answer to that."

"Which is?"

"I already have a twin brother."

"And?"

"There's room for improvement, but he's . . . okay."

I laughed. "I have a twin sister—and she's exactly the same way."

And she said, "Fair enough."

I was about to leave the room when she said, smiling, "Another thing."

"What?"

"Della wants to be fixed up with one of your band friends."

"Which one?"

"She doesn't care. Just not Stuart."

40.

MEG

● ○

Edward and I just had a bit of a conversation about what happened. He and I are the only ones who really know, though I get the sense neither of us has the full story. But we did laugh together a little, second day in a row. That was nice. Though I forgot to ask him about that kid who said she was his girlfriend. Who was that?

He went out skateboarding. He invited me, but I said no thanks. I wanted to think some more about everything that happened, figure it out, piece it together, maybe write it all down in my journal.

I picked up my pencil and journal and tried to figure out where to start, how it all started. Out of habit I started to list for myself all the things that were wrong with me, but then I ripped the page out of my journal and tore it up into little pieces. No great loss: I have that list memorized anyway, and I didn't feel like going over it again. Too boring. True, I have frizzy hair, an infinite tundra of a forehead, an unflat stomach, etc., etc., but for my as-yet never-written list of not-so-horrible parts of me, I'd finally come up with one thing: I can laugh at myself. *I may be crazy, but at least I know it* might not balance out brilliant or pretty, and it might not get me that spot on the *Today Show*, either, but hey, I'm not that much of a morning person anyway.

So for now I'm just staring out the window, having a good laugh at my own expense. I've been here since everybody went to bed last night and I washed all that makeup off my face and took off the Big Bird suit. I swear my body expanded an inch and a half when released. It felt so good to pull on my schlumpy old sweats. I considered surfing channels or reading or getting something accomplished, but instead I just sat here in the big leather chair, watching the darkness brighten as the night turned into day.

It reminded me of Mom's favorite expression: "The twins are like night and day."

Yup, I guess that is us. Night and day. Though I can't figure out which is which anymore.

Never mind!